I0661986

William Lockhart

The conversion

Of Marie-Alphonse Ratisbonne

William Lockhart

The conversion
Of Marie-Alphonse Ratisbonne

ISBN/EAN: 9783741189005

Manufactured in Europe, USA, Canada, Australia, Japa

Cover: Foto ©Andreas Hilbeck / pixelio.de

Manufactured and distributed by brebook publishing software
(www.brebook.com)

William Lockhart

The conversion

THE
CONVERSION

OF

MARIE-ALPHONSE RATISBONNE:

ORIGINAL NARRATIVE OF

BARON THÉODORE DE BUSSIÉRES;

FOLLOWED BY A LETTER

FROM MR. RATISBONNE TO REV. MR. DUFRICHE-DESGENETTES
CURÉ OF NOTRE-DAME DES VICTORIES AT PARIS.

———

EDITED BY THE REV. W. LOCKHART,
OF THE ORDER OF CHARITY.

NEW YORK:
P. J. KENEDY,

PUBLISHER TO THE HOLY APOSTOLIC SEE,
EXCELSIOR CATHOLIC PUBLISHING HOUSE,
3 AND 5 BARCLAY STREET.
1897.

WHILE I affirm that all the facts contained in this narrative are related with rigorous exactness, and with the sincerest truth, I declare, in compliance with the decree of Urban VIII. that I believe them as facts resting simply on human testimony, and on motives of human reason alone.

THE BARON DE BUSSIÈRES.

Rome, *17th February*, 1842.

PREFACE.

We have given in this volume a literal translation of the original accounts of the conversion of M. Alphonse Ratisbonne. The attempt to construct an independent narrative would be presumptuous in itself, and would lose the simple force and freshness of these genuine documents. Those who know the scrupulous and almost suspicious care with which the pretensions of any alleged miracle are tested at Rome, will feel the value of the decree of the Cardinal-Vicar which is prefixed. Baron de Bussières prefaced his first edition with a declaration, that he claimed for his narrative only that measure of assent which may be granted to any ordinary statement, resting on human evidence alone; this decree has raised the conversion of Mr. Ratisbonne to the position of an accredited miracle.

It is both sad and strange to observe the air of superb disdain with which miracles such as this are set aside, even by those who seem least removed from the Church, and who profess to accept the miracles of Holy Scripture on their own evidence,

and to be familiar with the laws of moral reason
ing.

And yet, surely, those who reject this statement as an imposture or a delusion, should feel
bound to show wherein it lacks the criteria of a
true miracle. We may assume that they will be
unwilling to affirm that the power of working
miracles was restrained within the limits of the
apostolic age ; they know that this hypothesis is
fatal to historical Christianity, and belies the
promise of its inspired records. Nor will they
say that a miracle is so improbable a thing in the
kingdom of God that no amount of testimony
can render it credible; they know well, that on
this view, they could ha dly rescue the miracles
of the Gospels from the hands of unbelievers.

They must rest their rejection on one of these
grounds : they either regard the evidence for this
particular miracle as insufficient or untrustworthy ;
or they shrink from doctrines and practices which
seem to them imbedded in it, or presupposed by it.

Yet they have learnt from a great authority amongst themselves,* that objections
to any revelation from God, as distinguished from objections to its evidence, are
frivolous. It is not competent to them to set
aside credible testimony to a miracle, simply
because that miracle carries with it theologi-

* _Butler's Analogy_, Part II. ch. iii.

cal consequences which they deem at variance
with the general scheme of religion. Nor would
they thus reserve any right to blame the Jews for
rejecting our Lord's miracles. The only question
which they can logically entertain is the evidence
for this particular miracle—the apparition of the
Blessed Virgin to Alphonse Ratisbonne in the
church of St. Andrea at Rome.

And if we weigh the character of the witness
and his competency; the improbability of his being deceived or wishing to deceive; the simple
fact of the entire change wrought upon him in a
moment, in the conversion of his heart and the il-
lumination of his mind; the consequences of his
testimony to himself; and then, the many years
which have tested his sincerity and his stability;—
if we weigh all these circumstances, we may ask
whether it is possible to decline to receive his testimony on any grounds which would not excuse
the Jews that dwelt at Damascus for refusing to
credit the conversion of Saul of Tarsus, and Fes-
tus for deeming him mad. We repeat, that those
who feel that there is no antecedent improbability in the occurrence of miracles, that the later
miracles cannot be discredited on *à priori* grounds
without shaking the credit of those of the Gospels, are bound to justify their rejection of this
miracle by impeaching its evidence. This is the
only issue which a Christian can properly raise;
and that testimony cannot be trivial or in-
1*

different which the Church has stamped with the
seal of its acceptance.

But here we would invite attention to some
weighty and suggestive remarks of Cardinal Wiseman, in his review of a pamphlet entitled *A Voice
from Rome.**

"In proof that the Blessed Virgin is worshipped as the
Mother of mercies, temporal and spiritual, the author before
us appeals to the Baron de Bussières' account of M. Ratisbonne's conversion from Judaism, 'which he distinctly attri-
butes to the immediate operation of the Virgin Mary; for he
relates, that it was effected by her actual appearance to him.'
Now, what is meant to be granted, and what is meant to be
doubted here, we do not know. We suppose that no one
doubts that M. Ratisbonne, from a Jew, did become a Catholic, and has become a religious; having abandoned home and
friends, and given up a long-cherished alliance. Any one
might as well deny that Sir R. Peel is prime minister. That
he went into the church of St. Andrew a Jew, and came out
a Christian, is attested upon evidence as certain as any fact
can well be—that of trustworthy and honest men, who saw
him and spoke with him before and after. For the change
something must account. That it was a *true* conversion from
Judaism to Christianity, with great temporal sacrifices, is
clear; and such a conversion must have been the work of divine grace. How communicated is the question. The only
witness can be the convert. He tells us that it was through
an apparition of the Mother of God, who instructed him in the
mysteries of our holy religion. Are we to believe that a person is chosen by the Divine Goodness for an object of a most

* *Dublin Review*, Dec. 1848. Cardinal Wiseman's Essays, vol. I. 550.

singular act of grace, at the moment that he devises and tells
an abominable falsehood, to rob Him of the glory of it, and
give it to another, by feigning a vision of the Blessed Virgin?
What does the author of the *Voice* mean to throw doubt on?
on the apparition, as for such a purpose impossible? or on the
consequences drawn from it? Surely not on the latter; for if
the vision was true, it was right to consider the blessed Mother
of God, not as the *source*, but as the *channel*, of a great
'spiritual mercy.'

"If he wish to insinuate that it would be derogatory to
God's honour, or incompatible with His revealed doctrines, to
believe such a mode of communicating grace and religious
instruction possible, and consequently, that the whole must be
a figment or a delusion, we will, in answer, relate another
similar story, in which not a Jew, but a bishop, was the
party; and we will premise that we have it on the best authority.

"The person to whom we allude was a young man of singular piety and virtue. Left young an orphan, he devoted his
youth to study in a celebrated university. There his assi-
duity in learning was surpassed only by the purity and innocence of his life, which stood the test of severe trials, and escaped the snares laid for him by profligate companions, jealous
of his virtue. Having made himself master of all profane
learning, he entered on a course of sacred studies, under the
most celebrated professor of the day, and soon made considerable progress. He was, however, while yet young, put into
orders, and even named bishop, before he considered himself
well enough grounded in theological knowledge; though
probably his humility led him to exaggerate his deficiencies.
He found himself quite unequal to the task of preaching the
Divine Word; and on the eve of his first undertaking this
duty, he lay sleepless on his bed, in agitation and anxiety.
Suddenly he saw before him a venerable figure of an old

man, whose countenance, attitude, and garb, bespoke great
dignity, but who, at the same time, appeared most gracious
and affable.   Terrified at this appearance, he leaped from his
couch, and respectfully asked who he was, and for what purpose he had come.   The old man replied, in a gentle voice,
that he had come to calm his doubts and solve his difficulties.
This declaration soothed his fears, and made him look towards
his visitor with a mixture of joy and awe ; when he perceived,
that by steadily pointing with his hand towards the other side
of the apartment, he seemed to wish to turn his attention in
that direction.   Thither he consequently turned his eyes, and
there he beheld a lady of peerless majesty, and of more than
human beauty, so resplendent that his eyes could not bear the
brightness of the vision, but he must needs bend them and his
countenance down, in reverential awe.   Thus he listened to
the conversation of these two heavenly beings, which fully
instructed him on the subjects whereon he felt anxious, and
at the same time informed him who his gracious visitors were.
For the lady, addressing the other by the name of the Evan-
gelist John, requested him to instruct the youth in the mystery of heavenly piety ; and he replied, ' that he was ready to
do even this, to please the Mother of his Lord, seeing that she
desired it.'   And accordingly he did so.

   "Such is our counterpart to the narrative objected to by
our author, respecting M. Ratisbonne's conversion.   Now, before giving the name of our authority for this wonderful history, or of the person to whom it refers, we will only beg our
reader, if not sufficiently versed in ecclesiastical biography, at
once to answer both points, to say to what Church or religion
he considers either the writer or the subject of this anecdote
belongs.   Could he believe us, if we told him that it happened to Bishop Ken, or Bishop Wilson, or Archbishop Laud ;
or that we had transcribed it, as gravely told by some Angli-
can clergyman in a life of any of them ?   We are sure he

could not. The idea of a Protestant Bishop learning his
faith from a vision of the Blessed Virgin, would be deemed re-
pugnant to every principle and every feeling of the religion.
But were we to tell the reader that the bishop spoken of was
St. Alphonsus Liguori, or even St. Charles, and the narrator
an Italian monk or priest, he would at once allow, that such
an account, from such a pen, concerning such a person, was
perfectly consistent with the principles of both; and though, if
a Protestant, he might declare that he did not believe the
story, he would acknowledge that it did not surprise him to
find it in such a place. It must, then, be a Catholic, and not
a Protestant, who thought or said he saw such a vision; and
it must be a Catholic, and not a Protestant, who has recorded
it, as believing it. And so it was. The bishop who thus
learnt his faith was St. Gregory Thaumaturgus, only little
more than two hundred years after Christ; and ‘the recorder
of the vision is the brother of the great St. Basil, St. Gregory,
Bishop of Nyssa. This would have been a nice anecdote for
our ancient note-taker upon the doctrines of Catholics."

The real reason why miracles such as this are
rejected with scorn, or passed by with indifference,
is not their antecedent improbability nor the inade-
quacy of their evidence; it is that they imply and
render sensible the position and power of the blessed
Mother of God. The Protestant cannot endure
that glad and graceful vision of the Mother of Divine Grace—*radios evibrans misericordiæ suæ*—
as Catholic piety delights to image her. It is an
offence to him. It is something so intolerable to
him, that, in his antipathy, he forgets all canons of
moral reasoning; his conceptions and definitions

become confused, and he all'ws this consoling vision
to neutralise the positive evidence, that the Church
which discloses it is alone of God.

And yet waving in thought what we can never
forget in fact, that clear voice of the Church which
is the Catholic's warrant of faith, why should it be
thought a thing so violently incredible that the
Mother of God should occupy the position, and exercise the powers, ascribed to her by the Church ?
Surely there can be no natural and necessary improbability in that which East and West combine to
affirm. Except in the fancies of a modern and very
small section of the nominally Christian world, there
has never 'been any consciousness of an incompati-
bility between our assigned office and the Gospel.
Her glories and prerogatives, as Mother of Christians and a special channel of grace, have not shocked
the wisest and the holiest sons of the Church.

Nor can those who rightly ascribe so tremen-
dous an influence to Eve over the destinies of our
race, rightfully shrink from the range of power attributed by the Church to the advocate and counterpart of Eve. It cannot, surely, be a gratuitous
fancy to see in the effects of the unbelief and dis-
obedience of the mother of all living, in the order of
nature, a hint and a measure, though not a limit, of
the efficacy of the faith and obedience of the mother
of all living, in the order of grace.

But let us observe here, that the miraculous

element in the conversion narrated in this volume
is simply the apparition of the blessed Mother of
God, and not her intercessory power. The Catholic
regards that power as a supernatural fact, a law of
the spiritual kingdom, one of *the powers of the
world to come.* He needs no miracle to teach him
that. No number or splendour of miracles could
increase his faith in that. They would be but veri-
fications to sense of what he knows already, absolutely and infallibly, by the teaching of the Church;
what he sees already, by the deep intuition of faith.
Such a miracle as this might excite his faith, but
could not be its ground or warrant. He sees the
office and the prerogatives of the Blessed Virgin involved in the fact of the Incarnation. *Mary, of
whom was born Jesus*—he needs no more. Mary,
Mother of God; Mary, bequeathed to us as our
mother from the Cross: the Divine Maternity in-
cludes and implies all. Her glories and her mighty
powers are only its natural consequences, and its
fitting adornment.

Is he reminded of the absence of express command to seek her intercession? He feels that he
has the command of that same Spirit by whose inspiration Scripture was written. For the Church
can ever say, *it hath thus seemed good to the Holy
Ghost and to us.* He would remind the objector,
that the relation in which the Mother of God stands
to us being known, the duty of religious regard to

her, on Bishop Butler's principles, arises out of that
relation itself, and is an obligation of reason, bind-
ing as soon as that relation is known. It is our
duty as well as our privilege to seek the intercession of those who have power with God; and he
would call on the objector to produce some prohibi-
tion of so natural an exercise of that privilege.
And, indeed, Catholics feel that this objection does
strike at intercessory prayer in general. There is,
we know, an intercession, vast and mighty, which
rests upon and carries out, if we may so speak, the
great mediation of the Word made flesh; and that
mediation is a legitimate object of desire, and consequently of petition, to every Christian man. It
is for the objector to produce a command in limita-
tion of this our right, in the covenant of grace.

But then, to invoke the Blessed Mother, to imagine that she can hear our cry and turn on us her
pitying eyes—it is this which is deemed so absurd
as to need no refutation. As if the charge of absurdity did not recoil on those who, with gross
conceptions, impose on the world unseen the laws
of space and time and the like, which rule this
world that is seen; who dare to limit the range of
the perceptions of the blessed by the laws of man's
bodily senses, senses which are but the spirit's
points of contact with the material world. Surely,
it is both shallow and unscientific to reason from the
senses of *this body of our lowness*, to the powers

and perceptions of the saints who reign with Christ.
Be it so, that we know not precisely how the Saints
hear our invocations. It is enough, to turn the
force of this objection drawn from our ignorance,
to say that we can conceive many ways in which
they may know the desires of our hearts. It is
quite enough for the Catholic to say : what if

> A sea before
> The throne is spread ; its pure still glass
> Pictures all earth-scenes as they pass.
> We, on its shore,
> Share, in the bosom of our rest,
> God's knowledge, and are blest.

Still there is a jealousy, honourable in its motive, most unwise in its conclusions, that our recourse to the Blessed Mother of Christians does in
some way interfere with the simplicity of our trust
in Jesus. It is impossible for those who are without, to understand the practical and ever-present
safeguards of the Catholic from all error, from all
excess. They cannot know, for instance, the effect
of the Mass in regulating all his language and
thoughts ; nor how impossible it is that this perception of the greatness of the powers which God
does communicate to the creature, should lessen the
greatness, or dim the glory of those which are in
communicable. Surely it should suffice to affirm that
the sole Mediatorship of the Incarnate Son of God

2

is the very condition of all Catholic theology and
practice. Like the weakness of man and the might
of grace, it is a law of the spiritual order, every
where felt, every where presupposed, every where
taken for granted, underlying every statement,
pointing every prayer. It is not so much a part of
the Gospel, as the Gospel itself. But the intercession of the Blessed Virgin and of the Saints cannot
be so stated as to clash with this oneness of mediation. They cannot ask otherwise than in accord-
ance with His will, nor apart from His great
pleading. It is upon that golden altar, which is before the throne of God, that the prayers of all saints
are offered, in St. John's vision. Now this is ever
present to the Catholic. However largely he may
ask of our Blessed Mother—and he does ask largely
—the principle of his asking and the law of its in-
terpretation are, *Tu da, per precata dulcisona*—
by thy sweet prevailing prayer. However wide
and, to human notions unlimited, the range of
power he ascribes to the Mother of God, it abides
still an *omnipotentia supplex*, as St. Bernard beau-
tifully says. It cannot be otherwise to him. He
is never even tempted to confound the creatures
with the Creator, to mistake the streams for the
source.

    But, indeed, it is not the illumination of the
mind that is needed to bring back the strayed sheep
to the fold; it is the attraction of the heart and

the bending of the will, and this is the work of God
alone. Would those who doubt and object but
meditate awhile on the solitary prerogative of Mary,
on her proximity to the flesh of Jesus, and on the
intensity of the mutual love that must bind together that Son and that Mother; would they but
try to look at her revealed position from the
Church's point of view, with all those limitations
and checks and safeguards of which they can form
no notion; would they do this, not with the hard
cold gaze of the intellect, but with a loving docile
heart; the objections which now hang like clouds
before their soul's eye would melt away of themselves and leave no trace. To such a one we would
say, in all affection, if you must reason ere you believe, remember the laws which control all moral
reasoning; remember that no number of even irre-
ducible objections are of weight against that which
rests upon direct and positive evidence; remember
that though this evidence is " liable to objections,
and may be run up into difficulties, it is not lost in
these difficulties or destroyed by these objections;" *
remember that those who, like St. Bernard, St. An-
selm, St. Bonaventura, St. Alphonsus, have been
most devout to Mary, have spoken of Jesus with
the tongues of angels rather than of men; and
pray—*ora fortiter et fideliter.* And as you gaze,

* *Butler's Analogy,* Part II chap. vi.

you will see how the Mother of Jesus is the mother of His mystical body likewise—*Mater membrorum Ejus*, as St. Augustine speaks. As you fathom the import of the words, *Behold the handmaid of the Lord*, you will come to feel that it is a mighty plea and an availing, to say, *Behold, O Lord, how that I am Thy servant, and the son of Thine handmaid;* and you will soon be enabled to continue the words of the psalm, *Thou hast broken my bonds asunder.*

We owe an apology to our Catholic readers for the length to which these remarks have extended. *You* can hardly grasp the reality of the difficulty which Protestants feel in the intercession of the Blessed Virgin and of the Saints. You can scarcely believe that men, believing the mystery of the Incarnation, can really confound things so accordant indeed, yet so distinct, as the affiance of a Christian in Christ, and his recourse to the prayers of all saints, without intellectual weakness or moral perversity. To you the miracle related here is, if I may so speak, quite natural and in keeping; wonderful indeed, but still what you are prepared to expect from the Mother of mercy.

To you all Scripture speaks of her, in type and figure, in prophecy and promise. To you the Incarnation is unintelligible apart from her, and doctrine heterodox or unmeaning which makes no mention of her. You know that as you have loved

Jesus more, you have felt for her whom He loved
best on earth, whom He cannot but delight to honour
in heaven—a truer, deeper, more loyal, and more
trustful love; and that as your devotion to the
Mother of God has gathered strength, you have
known and loved Jesus with a less reserved and
less reserving love. You know and feel that God
has indeed done great things unto her; but it has
never occurred to you that He has thereby dimmed
the glory of His name. You have rather said with
her—*et sanctum nomen Ejus.*

This narrative is of conversion, of Mary's tender
pity towards those who know her not. How can we
better express our thankfulness for this instance of
her compassion than by praying for those to whom
that very compassion is an offence and a hindrance?
We know, by manifold experience—*we have heard
with our ears, and our fathers have declared it
to us*—the reality, the range, and the patience of
that compassion. Let us pray for those who, from
amidst their gathering gloom, are casting wistful,
timid looks towards the one unwavering light, that
God's grace may still lead them on, and gently clear
their way through their thorny objections, until it

> brings them under Mary's smile
> And Peter's royal feet.

2*

Decree verifying and accrediting the Miraculous Conversion of MARIE-ALPHONSE RATISBONNE.

In the name of God.   Amen.

IN the year of our Lord and Saviour Jesus Christ one thousand eight hundred and forty-two, being the fifteenth of the Roman Indiction, and the twelfth year of the Pontificate of our Holy Father Pope Gregory XVI., and on the third day of June.

In the presence of the Very Eminent and Reverend Constantine Cardinal Patrizi, Vicar-General of our Holy Father the Pope, Ordinary Judge of the Roman Court . . . . appeared the Very Reverend Francis Anivitti, Proctor-Fiscal of the tribunal of the Vicariate, who had been specially deputed by the Very Eminent and Reverend the Cardinal-Vicar, to make inquiry and to examine witnesses in regard of the truth and reality of the wonderful conversion from Judaism to the Catholic Religion, granted, through the intercession of the Blessed Virgin Mary, to Alphonse Ratisbonne, a native of Strasburg. twenty-eight years of age, and now present in this city: the which Proctor declares that he applied himself to the inquiry intrust-

In Dei Nomine.   Amen.

ANNO a salutiferâ D. N. J. C. Nativitate milles. octogentes. quadragesimo secundo, Indict. Rom. XV., Pontificatus autem sanctissimi D. N. PP. Gregorii XVI. ann. XII. die vero tertiâ Junii.

Coram Eminentissimo ac Reverendissimo Constantino Card. Patrizi, sanctissimi D. N. PP., in almâ urbe Vicario-Generali, Romanæque curiæ ejusque districtus Judice Ordinario . . . . . . comparuit Reverendissimus D. Franciscus Anivitti, Promotor Fiscalis tribunalis Vicariatus, ab eodem Eminentissimo ac Reverendissimo D. Card. Vicario specialiter delegatus, ad effectum inquirendi et examinandi testes super veritate et relevantiâ mirabilis conversionis ab Hebraismo ad Catholicam religionem, quam, intercedente B. V. Mariâ, obtinuit Alphonsus-Maria Ratisbonne, Strasburgensis, anno viginti octo, in urbe præsens ; dixitque muneri sibi demandato, alacri libentique animo suscepto, quâ potuit sedulitate ac diligentiâ satisfacere studuisse, ed to him with the utmost care and diligence, and with a ready and willing mind. He declares further, that he has submitted the witnesses, to the number of nine, to a formal examination, and that they all display a marvellous agreement in their account of the alleged fact, and of its consequences and results. Whereupon he declared that, in his judgment, nothing was wanting in the characteristics of a true miracle; but that, nevertheless, he referred the decision of the question to his Eminence, and besought him to issue a definitive decree, as it might seem to him expedient in the Lord, after a full examination of the acts and documents laid before him.

Whereupon the Very Eminent and Reverend Cardinal-Vicar, having received the report, and read the questions proposed to the witnesses, together with their answers; and after mature and careful consideration of the same, after having also taken the advice and judgment of theologians and other holy men, in the form required by the Council of Trent, Session 25, *de invocatione*, &c., pronounced and declared definitively, that he affirmed the reality and truth of the miracle wrought by God, at the intercession of the Blessed Virgin Mary, in

subjiciendo formali examini numero novem testes, qui, omnes ad fiscalia interrogatoria respondentes, ingenuâ enarratione, in iis quæ ad substantiam facti et mirabilis eventus extrema pertinent, mire concordant. Quamobrem sibi visum esse asseruit, nihil ad rationem veri miraculi ulterius posse desiderari. Rem tamen omnem definiendam remisit Eminentiæ suæ Reverendissimæ, quæ, visis et examinatis actis, examinibus et documentis, definitivum decretum prout in Domino expedire ei videbitur, interponere dignabitur.

Et tunc Eminentissimus ac Reverendissimus D. Card. in urbe Vicarius, auditâ relatione, viso processu, visis testium examinibus, juribus, ac documentis, iis sedulo matureque consideratis, consultationibus etiam requisitis theologorum aliorumque piorum virorum, juxta formam Concilii Tridentini, Sess. 25, de invocatione, veneratione, et reliquiis sanctorum, ac sacris imaginibus, dixit, pronuntiavit, et definitive declaravit, plene constare de vero insignique miraculo, a D. O. M. intercedente B. Mariâ Virgine, patrato, videlicet instantaneæ the instantaneous and perfect conversion from Judaism of Alphonse Ratisbonne aforesaid. And, inasmuch as it is *honourable to confess and reveal the works of God*, his Eminence is pleased to permit that this narrative be printed and published, and held as authentic, for the glory of God, and for the increasing the devotion of all true Christians to the Blessed Virgin Mary.

Given at the palace of the aforesaid Very Eminent and Reverend Cardinal-Vicar and Ordinary Judge, on the day, month, and year aforesaid.

C. CARD. Vicar.
CAM. DIAMILLA, Notary,
JOSEPH, Chancellor.
TARNASSI, Secretary.

A true copy.

✠

Place of the seal.

perfectæque conversionis Alphonsi-Mariæ Ratisbonne ab Hebraismo. Et quoniam opera Dei relevare et confiteri honorificum est (Tob. xii. 7), ideo ad majorem Dei gloriam, et ad augendam devotionem Christi fidelium erga B. Virginem Mariam, benigne in Deo concessit, ut præfati insignis miraculi relatio publicis typis tradi, impressaque evulgari possit, et valeat.

Datum ex ædibus ejusdem Eminentissimi D. Cardinalis, urbis Vicarii et Judicis Ordinarii, die, mense et anno quibus supra.

C. CARDIN., Vicarius
CAM. DIAMILLA, Not. Deput.
JOSEPH, Can.
TARNASSI, Sec.

Concordat cum originali.

✠

Loco signilli.

THE CONVERSION

OF

MARIE-ALPHONSE RATISBONNE.

"*Et omnis plebs, ut ridit,
dedit laudem Deo.*"

HE who made use of a little clay from the
way-side to open to the light of heaven the eyes
of him that had been born blind, permitted
me to be the chief witness of an event of
which human reason alone can render no ade-
quate account. The fact I am about to relate
is beyond dispute. I am to speak of what I
saw with my own eyes—of what a multitude
of competent and trustworthy witnesses con-
firm—a man, in full possession of all his
senses and faculties, entered a church an obstinate Jew; and, by one of those swift flashes
of grace which laid Saul prostrate at the gates
of Damascus, he came forth, ten minutes afterwards, a Catholic in heart and in will.

Towards the close of the autumn of 1841,

a young man, connected with a distinguished
family at Strasburg, arrived at Naples. He
was on his way to the East, in quest of health
and pleasure : yet it was not without regret
that he had quitted his native city ; for he left
behind him a fair and gentle girl whom he
loved with tender affection, and in whom his
heart had stored up its rich treasure of hope.
She was his own niece; but mutual affection,
no less than family reasons, had determined
their union.

Alphonse Ratisbonne was a Jew; he was
destined, to all appearance, to a brilliant position in the world, and had resolved to devote
himself to the great work of the *regeneration* of
his co-religionists. His thoughts and aspira-
tions all revolved around this one high
purpose, and his wrath kindled at every thing
that reminded him of the curse that rests
upon the descendants of Jacob. Fifteen years
before the time of which I am speaking, and
while he was yet a child, his heart had been
wounded in one of its most sensitive affections.
Theodore Ratisbonne, his brother, became a
Catholic, and received holy orders. Time had
been powerless to close this wound ; his hatred
deepened year by year, and he studiously fo-
mented the deadly resentment of his family.

The blue sky of Naples could not make
him forget the East, the object of his journey,
nor the joys that awaited him on his return.
But a few months remained, and Sicily, Malta,

and Constantinople were to be visited. The summer of 1842 was to restore him to his home, and to witness a union which would fix his position in life, and assure his perfect happiness : it was time to be going. So he went out one morning to take his place in the steamer for Palermo. On his way it struck him that he had not seen Rome; that if he returned to Strasburg, and married, and became involved in the cares of business, there was but little likelihood of his ever revisiting Italy; and under the influence of this sudden thought he turned aside into the stage office took his place, and within three days found himself in Rome.

His stay was to be very short. His plans were all made; in a fortnight he would return to Naples. It was all in vain that the Eternal City displayed her wonders before him, he could not spare a day more; the East and his bride awaited him. So he set to work like a true tourist; visited ruins, churches, and galleries, and crowded his memory with a confused medley of impressions. He was eager to have done with this city, to which he had been drawn by an unaccountable fascination rather than by an intelligent curiosity.

And now he has finished his rounds. He starts for Naples to-morrow; but he must pay a farewell visit to an old friend. Gustave de Bussières had been his schoolfellow; and they had kept up their early friendship, in

spite of the antagonism of their religious opinions. My brother Gustave is a very zealous
Protestant, of the sect of the Pietists. He
had made sundry attempts to gain over the
young Israelite; but their discussions usually
wound up with two expressions, which sufficiently indicate the position and temper of the
disputants : *Fanatical Protestant,* shouted the
one : *Callous Jew,* retorted the other.

Ratisbonne did not find my brother at
home, and so he came on to me. But he had
resolved not to come in ; he would merely
leave a farewell card. Chance, or rather
Providence, ordered it so that his knock was ·
answered by an Italian servant, who mistook
his meaning, and introduced him, to his great
annoyance, into the drawing-room.

We had met but once, at my brother's,
and notwithstanding all my efforts, I had
failed to obtain from Ratisbonne any thing
beyond the cold civility of a well-bred man.
However, he was Gustave's friend ; he was
the brother of my own dear friend, the Abbé
Ratisbonne ; and so I received him cordially,
talked to him of the wonders around him, and
gradually elicited his impressions of Rome.

"A rather odd thing happened to me the
other day," said he, in passing ; "while I was
looking over the church of Aracœli on the
Capitol, I felt myself suddenly seized with an
emotion for which I could assign no cause.
The *valet de place,* seeing my agitation, asked

me what was the matter, and whether I would
go out into the open air; adding, that he had
often seen strangers similarly affected."

While Ratisbonne was telling me this, I
suppose that my glistening eyes seemed to
say to him, *You will be a Catholic;* for he
went on to say, with a marked intention, that
this emotion was not at all specifically Christian, but purely religious, in the most general
sense of the word. " Besides," he continued,
" as I came down from the Capitol a melancholy spectacle rekindled all my hatred of
Catholicism : I passed through the Ghetto ;
and as I beheld the misery and the degradation of the Jews, I said to myself that, after
all, it was a loftier thing to be on the side of
the oppressed than on that of the oppressors."
Our conversation now began to take a contro-
versial turn ; I tried, in my eager fervour, to
impart to him my own Catholic convictions ;
but he only smiled at my efforts, said that he
felt a sincere pity for my superstition, and
that *he was born a Jew, and a Jew he would
die.*

At this point of our discussion there came
into my head a very extraordinary idea, suggested doubtless from above, for the wise of
this world would have called it foolishness ;
I said :

" Since you are so confident in the strength
and stability of your understanding, promise
me to wear something that I will give you."

"Let me see it first; what sort of thing is it?"

"Only this medal," said I, and I held up to him a medal of the Blessed Virgin, at sight of which he threw himself back in his chair, with a gesture of mingled indignation and astonishment.

" But," said I, quietly, "from your point of view it must be perfectly indifferent to you, whereas it would give me the very greatest pleasure."

" Oh, I will not refuse you," he exclaimed, with a hearty laugh; "I shall at least show you that people have no right to accuse us Jews of obstinate and insurmountable infatuation. Besides, you are furnishing me with a charming chapter for my notes and impressions of my travels." And he went on with a succession of jests which wrung my heart, for to me they were so many blasphemies.

However, I threw round his neck a ribbon to which one of my daughters had attached the blessed medal while we were talking. And now there remained a point still more difficult to gain. I wished him to recite S. Bernard's pious invocation, *Memorare, o piissima Virgo....* But this was too much for him; he refused very decidedly, and in a tone which seemed to say : Really, this man's impertinence is beyond all bounds. Still an interior force urged me on, and I combated his reiterated refusals with the energy of desperation. I held out the prayer to him, and begged him to take it away with him, requesting him to be kind enough to write it out for me, as I did not possess another copy of it.

At length he yielded, as if to rid himself of my importunity, and said, in a tone of vexation and contempt, "Well, I will write it out; you shall have my copy and I will keep yours;" and then he withdrew, muttering as he went, "What an unreasonable fellow that is! I wonder what he would say, if I were to plague him thus to make him recite some of my Jewish prayers!"

After he was gone, my wife and I looked at each other some time without speaking a word. Distressed by the blasphemy to which we had been compelled to listen, we united in imploring pardon from God for him, and we charged our two little daughters to say an *Ave Maria* at night for his conversion.

From this point every circumstance seems so important in order to the clear setting forth of this great work of God, that I feel it a duty to relate, as minutely and as accurately as I can, every thing that passed, from the day when Ratisbonne carried away the *Memorare* to the moment when the Mother of Mercy removed the veil which obstructed his soul's vision, and he received the grace to make a public profession of the Catholic faith.

At first Ratisbonne could not get over

his astonishment at my importunity : he, however, copied out the prayer; he read it and read it again, in order to aiscover what could give it such worth in my estimaticn, and why I ascribed to it so mighty an effi- cacy. By dint of writing and reading it he had got it by heart; it recurred to his memory continually; he went about repeating it me- chanically, just as we unconsciously hum an air which has struck our fancy.

I, on my part, felt entirely absorbed in this result of my interview with a man of whom I knew next to nothing, and with whom I had conversed that day for the first time. I could not account for the internal force which impelled me towards him, and which inspired me with a deep inexplicable convic- tion that God would, sooner or later, open his eyes. I resolved to prevent, at all hazards, his departure from Rome. I went to pay him a visit at the Hôtel Serny ; and as he was not within, I left a note for him, requesting him to call on me on the following day, which was Sunday, at about half-past ten in the morning.

In the evening it was my turn to watch before the Blessed Sacrament, according to he pious custom at Rome, in company with Prince M. A. B., and some other friends. begged them to join me in my prayers to ob tain of God the conversion of a Jew.

Ratisbonne came punctually at the hour appointed, and said to me, in an off-hand way, "Well, I hope you have forgotten your yesterday's dreams. I am come to say good-bye to you; I am off to-night."

"My dreams! the thoughts which you are pleased to call dreams occupy me more than ever; and as to your going away, we will not speak of that, for you must absolutely put it off for a week."

"Oh, that is impossible; I have taken my place."

"What of that? We will go together to the office to say that you have changed your mind and are not going."

"Oh, now this is going too far; most de cidedly I leave to-night."

"Most decidedly you will not leave to-night, even if I have to lock you up in my own room."

And then I went on to tell him that he could not leave Rome without having seen some grand ceremony at St. Peter's; that in a very few days he would have a very favourable opportunity; and, in short, he was so amazed at my pertinacity, that he suffered me to lead him off to the office to erase his name from the list of travellers; and then we visited the houses of the Augustinians and Jesuits.

I dined that same day at the Borghese palace, in company with the Count de Laferron-

3*

\
nays; and in the course of the evening I told
him the hopes that filled my own heart, and
earnestly commended my young Jewish friend
to his prayers. In the unreserved conversation that followed, M. de Laferronnays spoke
to me of the confidence he had always felt in
the protection of the Blessed Virgin, even at
the time when the cares and distractions of
political life had scarcely permitted that practical piety of which his later years offered so
edifying an example. "Keep up a good
hope," said he; "if he says the *Memorare*,
you have him to a certainty, and many others
with him."

Monday, January 17th, 1842.

I walked in different directions with Ratisbonne, who came to me about one o'clock.
I was grieved to notice the little fruit of our
conversations. He was still in the same dis-
position of mind—still hated Catholicism in-
tensely, and made the most disparaging
remarks about it—still parried by raillery,
arguments which he thought not worth the
trouble of serious refutation.

Mr. de Laferronnays died the same night
at eleven o'clock. He left to his sorrowing
friends and family the memory of an edifying
example, and the consoling hope that God
had called him thus because he was ripe for
heaven.* Having long loved him as my own

* At the end will be found some details of the last moments of this truly noble and Christian man.

father, I had my part not only in the sorrow
of his family, but in the mournful duties
which devolved upon them; yet the thought
of Ratisbonne followed me importunately even
beside the bier of my friend.

Tuesday, January 18th, 1842.

I had passed part of the night with this
sorrowing family, and felt unwilling to leave
them; yet my thoughts turned restlessly to
Ratisbonne, as though an unseen hand were
drawing me towards him. I did not wish
to leave the remains of my friend, but I
could not banish from my mind this soul
which 1 was so anxious to subdue to the
faith. I communicated my mental conflict
to the Abbé G., who had been for many
years the chaplain and the friend of M. de
Laferronnays. "Go," said he to me, "go
and carry on the work you have begun; in
doing so you will best fulfil the wishes of
our deceased friend, who prayed fervently
for the conversion of this young man."

I immediately ran after Ratisbonne, and
took possession of him; I showed him various
religious antiquities, that I might keep the
great truths of Catholicism in contact with his
mind. I got him to visit a second time the
church of Aracœ.i. If he felt any return of
his emotion it was very fugitive, for he listened coldly to me, and answered all my observations with witticisms. " I will turn over

these things in my mind," said he, "when I
am at Malta. I shall have plenty of time on
my hands, for I am to spend two months there,
and I shall be glad of any thing to keep me
from *ennui.*"

Wednesday, January 19th, 1842.

We walked in the direction of the Capitol
and Forum. Close by, on the Cœlian hill, is
the church of S. Stefano Rotondo, the walls of
which are covered with frescoes, which repre-
sent with terrible fidelity the various torments
of the early martyrs. Ratisbonne was horrified as we looked at them. "It is a hideous
sight," said he, as though to anticipate my
observations; "but those of your religion
were quite as cruel to the poor Jews in the
middle ages as the persecutors of antiquity
were to the Christians."

I showed him at St. John Lateran the bas-
reliefs above the statue of the twelve apostles.
On one side are the figures of the Old Testa-
ment, on the other their fulfilment in the
person of the Messias. The comparison seemed
to him ingenious.

We continued our walk towards the villa
Wolkonski. Ratisbonne was surprised at my
calmness; he could not reconcile it with my
eager desire for his conversion, and he remarked that he was more than ever a Jew. I
answered that I was full of confidence in the
promises of God, and that I was convinced

that, since he was honest and sincere, would one day be a Catholic, even if an angel from heaven were necessary to enlighten him.

We were then passing by the Scala Santa; I took off my hat, and pointing to my companion, said, "Hail, Scala Santa, here is a man who will one day ascend you on his knees." Ratisbonne burst into a fit of laughter, and we separated without my being able to indulge the feeblest hope that I had, in any degree, shaken his convictions. But I believed Him who hath said : *Knock, and it shall be opened to you.* I returned to pray beside the remains of my beloved friend; and as I knelt I asked him to aid in the conversion of my young friend, if, as I hoped, he had already attained the rest of the blessed.

Thursday, January 20th, 1842.

Ratisbonne has not made the slightest ad vance towards the truth; his will is inflexi ble as ever, he turns every thing into ridi cule, and seems to mind only earthly things About noon he went into a *café* on the Piazza di Spagna to read the newspapers. There he found my brother in-law, Edmund Humann; they chatted over the news of the day with a flippancy and an ease which excluded all idea of any serious preoccupation of mind.*

* It seems as if it had pleased Providence to order a...

It was about one o'clock. I had to make some arrangements at the church of S. Andrea delle Fratte for the ceremony of the morrow. But here is Ratisbonne coming down the Via Condotti; he will go with me, wait for me a few minutes, and then we will continue our walk. We entered the church. Ratisbonne noticed the preparations for a funeral, and asked for whom they were made. " For a friend I have just lost, and whom I loved exceedingly, Mr. de Laferonnays." He then began to walk about the nave, and his cold indifferent look seemed to say, "This is certainly a very ugly church." I left him on the epistle side of the church, to the right of a small enclosure destined to receive the coffin, and went into the convent.

I had only a few words to say to one of the monks—I wanted a tribune prepared for the family of the deceased; my absence could not have been more than ten or twelve minutes.

When I came back into the church I saw

things so as to exclude the possibility of doubt as to Ratisbonne's state of mind just before the unexpected grace of his conversion. About half-past twelve, as he came out of the café, he met his friend the Baron de Lotzbeck, and entered into conversation with him on matters the most frivolous. He spoke of dancing, of pleasure, of the fête given by Prince T. Had any one said to him at that moment, *Within two hours you will be a Catholic*, he would certainly have thought him out of his senses.

nothing of Ratisbonne for a moment; then I caught sight of him on his knees, in front of the chapel of S. Michael the Archangel. I went up to him, and touched him three or four times before he became aware of my presence. At length he turned towards me, his face bathed in tears; joined his hands, and said, with an expression which no words will render: " Oh, how this gentleman has prayed for me!"

I was quite petrified with astonishment; I felt what people feel in presence of a miracle. I raised Ratisbonne, I led him, or rather almost carried him, out of the church; I asked him what was the matter, and where he wished to go. "Lead me where you please," cried he; "after what I have seen I obey." I urged him to explain his meaning, but he could not; his emotion was too mighty and profound. He drew forth from his bosom the miraculous medal, and covered it with kisses and with tears. I brought him back to his apartment; and notwithstanding my repeated questions, I could get from him nothing but exclamations, broken by deep sobs: " Oh, what bliss is mine! how good is the Lord! what a fulness of grace and of happiness! how pitiable the lot of those who know not!" Then he burst into tears at thought of heretics and misbelievers. At length he asked me if I did not think him mad. " But no," he exclaimed,

"I am in my right senses; my God, my God, I am not beside myself; every one knows that I am not mad!"

This wild emotion became gradually more calm, and then Ratisbonne threw his arms around me and embraced me. His face was radiant, I might almost say transfigured; he begged me to take him to a confessor; wanted to know when he might receive holy baptism, for now he could not live without it; yearned for the blessedness of the martyrs whose sufferings he had seen depicted on the walls of S. Stefano Rotondo. He told me that he could give me no explanation of his state until he had received permission from a priest to do so; "for what I have to say," he added, "is something I can say only on my knees."

I took him immediately to the Gesù to see Father de Villefort, who begged him to explain himself. Then Ratisbonne drew forth his medal, kissed it, showed it to us, and exclaimed: "*I have seen her! I have seen her!*" and his emotion again choked his utterance. But soon he regained his calmness, and made his statement. I give it in his own words:

"I had been but a few moments in the church when I was suddenly seized with an unutterable agitation of mind. I raised my eyes, the building had disappeared from before me; one single chapel had, so to speak, gathered and concentrated all the light; and in the midst of this radiance I saw standing

on the altar lofty, clothed with splendours,
full of majesty and of sweetness, the Virgin
Mary, just as she is represented on my medal.
An irresistible force drew me towards her;
the Virgin made me a sign with her hand
that I should kneel down; and then she
seemed to say, That will do! She spoke not
a word, but I understood all."

Brief as this statement is, Ratisbonne could
not utter it without pausing frequently to take
breath, and to subdue the emotion with which
he was thrilling. We listened to him with a
sacred awe, mingled with joy and with gratitude, marvelling at the depth of the counsels
of God, and at the ineffable treasures of His
mercy. One word struck us especially by its
depth of mystery : *She spoke not a word, but
I understood all.* Indeed, it was quite enough
to listen to Ratisbonne; the Catholic faith
exhaled from his heart like a precious perfume
from the casket, which contains it indeed, but
cannot confine it. He spoke of the Real Presence like a man who believed it with all the
energy of his whole being; but the expression
is far too weak, he spoke like one to whom it
was an object of *direct perception.*

On leaving Father de Villefort, we went
to give thanks to God, first at S. Maria Maggiore, the favoured basilica of the Blessed
Virgin, and then at S. Peter's.

It is impossible to convey an idea of the
transport of Ratisbonne when he found him-

self in these churches. "Ah," said he to me, as
he warmly pressed my hands, " now I understand the love with which Catholics regard
their churches, and the piety which leads them
to embellish and adorn them ! ... How good
it is to be here ! one would long to go no more
out for ever ! ... it is earth no longer, it is the
vestibule of heaven."

At the altar of the Blessed Sacrament, the
Real Presence of Jesus so overwhelmed him
that he was on the point of fainting; and I
was obliged to lead him away, so awful did
it seem to him to appear before the living
God with the stain of original sin upon him.
He hastened to take refuge in the chapel of
the Blessed Virgin.* " Here," said he to me,
" I can have no fear; I feel myself under the
protection of an illimitable mercy."

He prayed with great fervour at the tomb
of the holy apostles. The history of the conversion of S. Paul, which I related to him,
made him shed tears abundantly.

He was astonished at the strength of the
posthumous bond, to use his own expression,
which united him to M. de Laferronnays; he
wished to pass the night beside his remains—
gratitude, he said, made it a duty. But Father
de Villefort, seeing that he was exhausted

---

* Many may be glad to remark, that M. Ratisbonne was
born in 1814, on the 1st of May, the month consecrated by
Catholic piety to the Mother of Divine Grace.

with fatigue, prudently opposed this pious desire, and advised him not to remain later than ten o'clock.

Ratisbonne then told us that the night before he had not been able to sleep; that he had always before his eyes a large cross, of a peculiar form, and without the image of our Saviour. "I made," said he, "incredible efforts to drive away this figure; but they were all fruitless." Some hours later his eye casually fell on the reverse of the miraculous medal, and he recognised his cross.

Meanwhile I was impatient to return to the family of M. de Laferronnays: I had such consolation to give them, at the moment when the venerated remains of him whom they bewailed were about to be taken from before their eyes. I entered the chamber of death in a state of agitation, I might almost say of joy, which at once attracted the attention of all present, and showed them that I had something of importance to communicate. They all followed me into an adjoining room, and I hastily related all that had passed.

I had brought them tidings from heaven. Their tears of grief were in a moment changed into tears of gratitude. These poor, smitten hearts could now bear with perfect Christian resignation that keenest of sacrifices, which death, exacts, the last farewell to the remains of him they had loved.

But I was eager to see again the son

whom God had just given me; he had begged
me not to leave him alone; he felt that he
needed a friend into whose heart he could pour
out the unfathomable emotions of such a day.

I asked him again and again the circumstances of the miraculous vision. He was
quite unable to explain how he had passed
from the right side of the church to the chapel,
which is on the left, and from which he was
separated by the preparations that had been
made for the funeral service. All he knew
was, that he had found himself suddenly on
his knees, and prostrate close to this chapel.
At first he had been enabled to see clearly
the Queen of Heaven, in all the splendour of
her immaculate beauty; but he could not
sustain the radiance of that divine light.
Thrice he had tried to gaze once more on the
Mother of Mercy; thrice he proved his in-
ability to raise his eyes beyond her blessed
hands, from which there flowed, in luminous
rays, a torrent of graces.

"O my God!" cried he, "I who but half
an hour before was blaspheming still! I who
felt a hatred so deadly of the Catholic religion!
. . . But all who know me know well enough
that, humanly speaking, I have the strongest
reasons for remaining a Jew. My family is
Jewish, my bride is a Jewess, my uncle is a
Jew. . . . In becoming a Catholic, I sacrifice
all the interests and all the hopes I have on
earth; and yet I am not mad—every one

knows that I am not mad, that I have never been mad! Surely they must receive my testimony."

Friday, January 21st, 1842.

The news of this signal miracle began to spread through Rome.* People were running from house to house, questioning one another, relating to one another the imperfect details they had been able to gather. It was all in vain that, with customary caution, they were on their guard lest they should receive a statement so startling on insufficient testimony. Doubt soon became impossible in presence of facts so evident and so notorious. Every one seemed to bless God for the privilege of being in Rome at a time when it had pleased Him to quicken our confidence in the immaculate Virgin, by attesting in so wonderful a way the power of her intercession. Every one longed to see and to question the thrice-happy youth, for whom the Mother of Divine Grace had descended from heaven to earth.

* Yesterday morning, as we were taking our c occhate in haste, before visiting *S. Agnese fuòri le Mure*, our good Monica came running in to tell us, in the joy of her heart, the news, *Un Ebreo è convertito !*—a Jew was converted yesterday ; yes, here, in our church of S. Andrea delle Fratre ! *Gesù mio! che bel miracolo !* We could not stay to hear more. In the evening this conversion was the topic of conversation at Cardinal Pacca's ; and this morning I heard all the details of this striking event. I met M. de Bussières in the *salon* of the Countess K., and he was good enough to relate to us what he has since published."—*Gaume ; les trois Rome,* ii. 173.

4*

I was with Ratisbonne at Father Villefort's, when General Chlapouski was introduced. "Sir," said he, "so you have seen
the likeness of the Blessed Virgin ; tell me all
about it."

"The likeness, sir!" cried Ratisbonne,
interrupting him ; "the likeness! I have seen
her herself, in reality, in her own person,
just as I see you there before me."

I cannot refrain from observing here, that
even if we can imagine an illusion in the
case of a person of Ratisbonne's character
and education, with prejudices so violent,
and with such interests both of affection and
of position, it could not have been produced
or aided by any outward representation ; for
in the chapel which was the scene of the
miracle, there is no statue, or picture, or
image of the Blessed Virgin, of any kind.

I was anxious now that Ratisbonne should
be introduced to the family of M. de Laferronnays. The most critical event of his
life was so bound up with the bereavement
which weighed so sorely upon them, that it
seemed but right that he should alleviate
their sorrow, by telling them with his own lips
of the tie of everlasting gratitude wherewith
it had pleased God to link his soul with that
of their departed one. But he was too much
affected to talk consecutively; he could do
little more than press with an indescribable
agitation the hands which were stretched out

to him, as to a brother or to a beloved child. " Oh, believe me, believe my words," said he repeatedly, when they questioned him; " it is to the prayers of M. de Laferronnays that I owe my conversion."

The new convert spent at my house the few days that passed before the retreat, in which he was to be prepared for his baptism. He read me some parts of his letters to his bride, to his uncle, to all the members of his family ; so that I was enabled to read his soul to its lowest depth. In our private conversations he recurred continually to the manifest proofs, which ought to convince the most sceptical, of the miraculous intervention by which his conversion was effected, and of his own perfect sincerity.

" The weightiest inducements," said he, "the strongest interests, bound me to my religion. A man has a claim to be believed when he sacrifices every thing to a conviction which must have come from heaven. . . If allithat I have stated is not rigorously true, I commit a crime, not only the most daring, but the most senseless and motiveless. In making my entrance into Catholicism by a sacrilegious lie, I not only risk my position in this world, but I lose my soul, and assume the frightful responsibility of all those whom my example may induce to do as I am doing. And what interest can I have in this? Alas, when my brother became a Catholic, and a

priest, I persecuted him with a more unrelent-
ing fury than any other member of my family.
We were completely sundered; I hated him
with a virulent hatred, though he had fully
pardoned me. At the time of my betrothal,
I said to myself that it was fitting that I
should be reconciled with my brother; I
wrote him a few cold lines, to which he returned an answer full of tenderness and of
charity. . . .

"One of my nephews died eighteen
months ago. My brother, the abbé, wished
to baptise him; when I knew it, I was in a
frenzy of rage. . . . I trust that God may send
me the severest of tests, that His own glory
may be advanced, and that the world may
know that I am sincere."

And surely we cannot question the sincerity and good faith of the man who, in his
twenty-eighth year, sacrifices all the joys of
his heart, all the hopes of his life, at the call
of conscience. For he knew well all the consequences of his resolution; he knew that
Christianity is the worship of the Cross;
again and again he had been told of the trials
which awaited him, and of the duties laid
upon him by the religion which he was so eager to embrace.

From the moment in which he requested
the sacrament of baptism, he was placed under the care of the venerable father who rules
a society justly dear to every Christian. This

good father, after hearing his story with his wonted benignity, and at the same time with calm gravity, had urged him to weigh well the sacrifices he would be compelled to make, the serious obligations he would have to fulfil, the peculiar conflicts which awaited him, the temptations and testing trials to which a step like his would expose him; and then, pointing to a crucifix which stood on the table, he said:

"That cross which you saw in your sleep, when once you have been baptised, you must not only worship it, but you must bear it;" and then, opening the Holy Scriptures, he turned to the second chapter of Ecclesiasticus, and read to Ratisbonne these words:

"Son, when thou comest to the service of God, stand in justice and in fear, and prepare thy soul for temptation. Humble thy heart and endure: incline thine ear, and receive the words of understanding: and make not haste in the time of clouds. Wait on God with patience; join thyself to God, and endure, that thy life may be increased in the latter end. Take all that shall be brought upon thee: and in thy sorrow endure, and in thy humiliation keep patience. For gold and silver are tried in the fire, but acceptable men in the furnace of humiliation. Believe God, and He will recover thee: and direct thy way, and trust in Him. Keep His fear, and grow old therein."

These divine words produced a deep im-

pression on Ratisbonne. Far from discour
aging him, they strengthened his resolution,
and gave him very serious and sober ideas
of Christianity. He listened, however, in silence; but at the close of the retreat which
preceded his baptism, he went in the evening
to see the holy priest who had read him these
words a week before, and begged for a copy
of them, that he might preserve them, and
meditate on them every day of his life.

Such are the facts which I submit to the
consideration of all thoughtful men. I have
related them artlessly, in their own simplicity, in all their truthfulness; for the edification of those who believe, for the instruction
of those who are yet seeking the place of
their rest. And happy shall I deem myself,
if, after having wandered long, too long, in
the gloom and amidst the contradictions of
Protestant sects, I may, by this simple narrative, excite in some erring brother the will
to cry, with the blind man in the Gospel,
Lord, that my eyes may be opened! for every
one who truly prays will soon have his eyes
opened to the sunlight of Catholic truth.*

* "My brother, two hours after his conversion, was seen
by Cardinal Mezzofanti, who was ready to throw himself on
his knees in adoration to God. Nothing was known of my
brother at Rome, and at first great apprehensions were entertained as to what his character might turn out to be. *He
had never read two pages of the Bible, never received any religious
instruction whatever*, was altogether of a light and superficial
character The Blessed Virgin appeared to him as close as I

THE BAPTISM.

Monday, January 31st, 1842.

Those whose privilege it was to obtain admission to the church of the Jesuits to-day, will not readily forget the ceremony which has completed that extraordinary event which still so profoundly affects the whole city, and which publicly authenticated one of those marvels of grace by which God would revive the faith of the lukewarm, and allure into the right way those who are yet walking in darkness.

M. Ratisbonne has made to-day, in presence of the Cardinal Vicar, his profession of the Catholic faith; he has received holy baptism, has been confirmed, and has made his first communion.

Long before the appointed hour the church of the Gesù, which had been chosen by the Cardinal Vicar for the ceremony, was filled with a pious crowd, eager to see this young Jew, whom the immaculate Virgin herself has

am to you; she made a motion to him that he should remain quiet under the divine influence. On rising out of his ecstasy, *he had received intuitively the knowledge of the Christian faith.* . . . I believe that he has more than once received a repetition of the grace he had at Rome, but I have never asked him on the subject. . . . My uncle is worth from six to seven millions of francs; he has disinherited my brother, who has renounced every thing.

"M. L'ABBÉ THÉODORE RATISBONNE."
Allies' Journal in France, p. 44.

deigned to bring to the foot of the cross.
There were present also many of those wandering sheep, those curious persons who long
to see every thing that is novel and striking;
but a contagious reverence pervaded the congregation, and all hearts were for a time
fused into a oneness of emotion by the interest and awe inspired by the distinguished
proselyte.

Prudent precautions had been taken to
preserve that degree of order which was necessary for the common edification of all.
The space between the altar of St. Ignatius
and that of St Francis Xavier was prepared
for the accommodation of the large assem-
blage; and although there were no places
reserved, the zeal of true Catholics had fore-
stalled the eagerness of the merely curious,
and thrown around the altar the protection
of their reverent silence and devout prayers.

About half-past eight M. Ratisbonne,
clothed in the white robe of a catechumen,
was led in by the reverend Father Villefort,
who had prepared him for baptism, and by
Baron Théodore de Bussières, his sponsor,
and took his place in the chapel of St. Andrew, near the principal entrance of the
church.* During the half-hour which fol-

* " To-day we took part in a ceremony, or rather an
event, the memory of which will never fade away from
my heart—the baptism of M. Ratisbonne. Ten days only
had passed since his conversion ; but the marvellous *neophyte*

lowed, he was naturally the object of general curiosity; but he endured with perfect resignation this severe test, so trying at a moment when his heart was heaving with the yearning presentiments of a new life. Fron. time to time he fervently pressed the rosary which he held in his hand, or gazed on the modal attached to it, as if to seek in the thought of her whose intercession had saved him, the strength and courage he so much needed.

At nine o'clock, his Eminence Cardinal Patrizi, Vicar of his Holiness, began to recite the prayers prescribed in the ritual for the baptism of adults. There are found psalms which seem as though they had been written expressly to clothe with words the feelings of the catechumen, and to tell out the way in which the Lord had been pleased to call him to the truth. For so wondrous is the depth of the Holy Scriptures, that every one finds in them the expressions which render most aptly the ever-varying experience of his soul, and the manifold circumstances of his inner life.

had *understood all*, and the illustrious Cardinal Mezzofanti, who is charged with the examination of catechumens, was amazed at the plenitude of light which the Father of lights had so instantaneously poured into this privileged soul.... What a spectacle! M. de Bussières, a converted Protestant, leading a Jew into the bosom of a Catholic Church! and what a Jew! a *jeune France* of eight-and-twenty, in all the fulness of his powers, his reason, and his self-will; but yesterday godless mocking, blaspheming, and to-day gentle as a lamb...."— *Gaume; les trois Rome*, ii. 220.

5

And what could paint more vividly the troubled and weary heart of the young Jew, as he beheld the enchantment pass away from the face of earth, and was sad amidst the pleasures of his favoured position? *Why art thou cast down, O my soul?* Poor stricken soul, in vain dost thou shift thine horizon, and seek the distraction of thy sadness in other and strange lands; still will *thy tears be thy bread day and night,* for there is no resting-place for the exile,—for day by day it is said to thee, in thy secret heart, *where is now thy God?* But *hope thou in God;* for soon shalt thou confess His Holy Name, and find the heart's true rest, the balm for every wound : *hope thou in God ; for I will still give praise to Him, the salvation of my countenance, and my God.* Think, that in His own appointed time He hath sent unto thee the Mother of mercies : *in the day-time the Lord' hath commanded His mercy.* Hope thou, then, in God; fear no longer to draw near unto the tabernacle of awe wherein lies hidden the Holy of Holies; say thou rather in thine heart, *and I will go in to the altar of God ;* He alone can slake my soul's deep thirst. Thou feelest now the hideousness of sin, of thine own inherited taint; *when shall I come,* when shall I enter the sacred ark, out of which is no salvation? when may I cast myself down before the face of my God? *when shall I come and appear before the presence of God?*

Like as the hart panteth after the fountains of water, so longeth my soul for the hallowed streams of baptism, so thirsteth my soul for God, the spring and fount of all strength and of all life.

When these preliminary prayers were sa. l. his Eminence proceeded in procession to the lower end of the church. There Father Villefort and M. de Bussières presented to him the young Jew. " What cravest thou of the Church of God ? " " Faith." And this faith, this holy Catholic faith, it was his already; the bright and morning star had already risen upon him, and enlightened him with its clear shining. And thus, when commanded to " detest the perfidy of the Jews, to put away with contempt the superstition of the Hebrews," he knew not a moment's hesitation, and the meek firmness of his replies showed that he was not unworthy of the boon the Church accorded him, in abridging for him the tests appointed for catechumens.

Already has the bishop breathed thrice upon him to put to flight the spirit of evil; he has marked him with the Christian's characteristic mark, the venerable sign of the cross, on his forehead, on his eyes, on his ears, on his breast, on his shoulders; in order to impress upon the new-born Chris tian that it was henceforth his duty to hallow to Christ his intelligence and his heart, and to bear with loving readiness the yoke of

the cross. He has given him to taste the
salt of wisdom, and has said over him the
prayers of exorcism. The neophyte is prostrate on the threshold of the temple—a
last, surest evidence of submission, a last,
unlooked-for test is applied, "Kiss the dust;"
and calmly and unhesitatingly he obeys.
There is no doubt that he is a Christian indeed,
for his heart has intuitively discerned that humility is the strait gate which leadeth to truth
and to salvation. Lesson of wondrous eloquence for us all, who are but too prone to
forget that Jesus our Master was *meek and
lowly in heart.*

There is no doubt; the *mind that was in
Christ* is in this candidate for Christ's service
too, for he is lowly and submissive. The
Church hesitates no longer; she looks upon
him, she treats him as her own beloved child.
She remembers no more his life in times past,
nor his blasphemies of yesterday ; she beholds
in him only the privileged child of Mary's
adoption. The bishop places the end of his
stole in his hand, in token of adoption, to
teach him that in the Catholic family the
children must lean trustfully on their fathers ;
and thus he leads, as in triumph, this beloved
sheep of the fold, snatched from the jaws of
the destroyer, to the altar of St. Ignatius.

But how shall we render justice to the
emotion of the congregation as Ratisbonne
passed before them? His face characterised

by a happy blending of decision and of gentleness, his long beard, his measured step, his white garment, every thing carried them back in thought to the days of the primitive Church —the Church of the catacombs.

Some worthy Roman women, who were crushing me in order to see more clearly, well expressed in their own simple way the brotherly charity which animated all who were present: *Ah, quanto sei caro! ah, beato lui!* and then they kissed their rosaries as if to thank the cause of our joy for this triumph of grace.

Then they pointed with affectionate curiosity to him whom God deigned to use to prepare His way before His face: "See he is a Frenchman—it was he who gave the medal to the Jew, who made him pray to the Blessed Virgin. *Ma che buon signore! che Dio le benedica!*" And we too repeated their words, and said in our deepest hearts: May God bless him, and all that are his!

And now the bishop is standing near the altar, and the catechumen kneels before him to receive the sacred waters of baptism. He is asked his name. "Marie," is his reply, with an outburst of gratitude and of love Marie! the thrice-blessed name of the Queen of Patriarchs, who has opened to him the gates of the Church, and will open for him those of heaven—the everlasting gates.

"What crave you?"

"Baptism."

5*

"Do you renounce the devil ?"

" I renounce him.

" And all his pomps ? "

" I renounce them."

" And all his works ? "

" I renounce them."

"Do you believe in God the Father Almighty, Creator of heaven and earth ? "

" I believe in Him."

" Do you believe in Jesus Christ His only Son our Lord, who was born and who suffered for us ? "

I believe in Him."

"Do you believe in the Holy Ghost, the Holy Catholic Church, the Communion of Saints, the remission of sins, the resurrection of the flesh, and the life everlasting ? "

" I do believe."

The tone and accent of deepest conviction with which this child of Mary pronounced this profession of the Catholic faith, produced on all present an impression which still thrills throughout their whole being.

" And now, what desirest thou ? "

" Baptism."

At length that sacred flood whose waters spring up unto everlasting life, has come down upon that brow so lowly bent; Marie Ratisbonne rises up a Christian,—a Christian pure and fervent as are the angels who stand about the throne of God.

He holds in his hand the blessed taper, whose flame betokens that light of submissive faith which wavers not nor misleads. The laying on of hands and the unction with holy chrism impart to him a second grace, in confirming the fulness of that which he has already received. Henceforward Ratisbonne is a disciple of the cross; he is prepared to confess aloud to all the faith of that Jesus who gave Himself for us.

And then M. l'Abbé Dupanloup* addressed to the congregation some of those glowing words which rise so readily from his heart when he has to tell of the goodness of our God, or of the loving power of Mary. We give a few fragments—fragments, alas! very incomplete and very weak —of this fervid *improvisation*. The sacred orator avowed before all his full and entire faith in the miraculous intervention of Mary, in the sudden conversion for which they were now blessing God; avoiding, as beseemed a submissive son of the Church, every expression which might even seem to anticipate the regular decision of the one only competent authority on a question of miraculous agency.

* Now Bishop of Orleans.

THE providence of God is wondrous in all its designs and in all its methods, and deeply are they to be pitied who can neither comprehend nor extol it. For them the life of man is but a mournful mystery; his days but a chain whose links are twined by fate; and man himself but a creature, noble indeed, but accursed in every faculty, thrust forth far from heaven upon this earth of tears and lamentation, to live in gloom, to die in despair, utterly forgotten by a God who heeds neither his virtues nor his sorrows... But, O my God, Thou art not thus unheeding, neither hast thou thus fashioned us; notwithstanding our profound and infinite misery, we are not to this extent miserable: Thy providence still keepeth watch over us; higher than highest heavens, deeper far and wider than the great and wide sea; it is an abyss unfathomable, of power, and wisdom, and of love. .... Thou hast made us for Thyself, O Lord, and our hearts are restless until they find rest in Thee. There is within us a sense of need, deep, infinite, which sways our whole souls, which devours us, ... and whenever we follow the instinctive tendency of this mighty want we surely find Thee.....
I bless Thee, above all, I adore Thee for that from Thy lofty and eternal dwelling-place

Thou dost remember, and remember with
compassion, the creatures Thy hand hath
formed; for that from Thy heavens Thou
dost design a look of pity and of love on
us, the lowliest product of Thine almighty
hand; for that, as saith the Prophet, Thou
dost shake the heavens and the earth, and
multiply Thy prodigies, in order to save
those whom Thou lovest so well.... to subdue to Thyself one solitary soul.....

And you, on whom every eye is now
turned with unutterable tenderness—for it
is God, it is the mercy of God, that we see
and love in you—you, whose presence here
inspires my thoughts—tell us what were your
thoughts and the ways of your heart,.....
by what hidden ways of mercy the Lord has
followed you, brought you back.....

For who are you? what is your petition
in this holy place? what homage do you come
to pay? what means that robe of stainless
white you bear? Tell us whence you came,
and whither your steps were bent? and what
power has so suddenly changed your pur-
poses?.... Tell us how, like Abraham, your
great ancestor,—Abraham, whose true son you
have this day become,—you were going on,
following the voice of the Lord, but not knowing whither you went; your eyes yet sealed
in darkness until you reached the Holy City.
..... The work of the Lord has not yet
reached its accomplishment; but it is yours to

tell us by what degrees the Sun of truth and
of justice arose upon your soul,—what was its
glowing dawn..... Why is it that you feel
with us, more keenly perhaps than we feel,
the good word of grace, the powers of the
world to come, and all our hopes so full of
blessedness?.... Tell us, for we have the
right to ask, why do you thus enter into our
possession, as into your own heritage? Who
has placed you thus at home in our midst? for
yesterday you were but a stranger and a so-
journer with us; we knew you not—or rather
we knew you.....

Here let me utter all; for I know what
joy I shall infuse into your heart in setting up
this memorial of your misery, and of the mercies of our God.

You loved not the truth, though He who
is the truth loved you; you resisted the efforts
of the most fervid and the purest zeal with a
smile of disdain, or a contemptuous silence,
or a subtle quibble, or a haughty demand of
overwhelming evidence, and, alas! with blas-
phemous jests. O God most patient! O Thou
who lovest us in spite of our sins and our miseries! Thy mercy has oftentimes a depth, a
sublimity, a tenderness, a might and a delicacy, which are to us infinite and incomprehensible.

Suddenly a rumour spreads throughout the
Holy City, and diffuses consolation throughout all Christian hearts. He who yesterday

was a blasphemer, who, even this very morning, ridiculed the friends of God—he preacheth
the Gospel—grace from above has been poured
upon his lips; from his mouth proceed only
blessing and words of gentleness; the keenest
light of faith has shone on his eyes; the unction of the Holy One has taught him all
things. Whence has he acquired those enlightened eyes of the soul, which see all,
which have *understood all?* O God, Thou art
good; Thy goodness is infinite; and I love to
repeat those gracious words which we heard
so recently from the blessed lips of him whose
memory can never fade away from our hearts;
—we made lamentation for him but a few days
since, but now we regret him indeed, yet we
cannot grieve for him: " Yes, Thou art good,
and the children of men have done well to
call Thee the *good* God." * Thou shakest the
laws of nature; Thou deemest nothing too
great for the salvation of Thy children. When
Thou comest not Thyself, Thou sendest Thine
angels. .... Thine angels, did I say?... O
my God, shall I speak? a reverent reserve
should close my lips—but *quœ est ista*—who
is this? Silence and speech are alike impossible.

Hail Mary, full of grace! and thou lovest
to shower down on us the plenitude of thy
mother's heart. *The Lord is with thee!* It

* The last words of M. de Laferronnays.

is through thee that He has been pleased to
come down even unto us. And now it behooves
me to borrow the kindling utterances of prophets, or to range the courts of heaven in quest
of images to set forth thy dignity and thy
praise. For, O Mary, thy name is sweeter to
us than earth's purest joy, sweeter than its
choicest odours, ravishing beyond the harmony of angels, *in corde jubilus;* sweeter to
the believing heart than the honeycomb to
the lips of the weary traveller, *mel in linguâ;*
more helpful and gentler to the guilty heart,
when it repents, than is the dew of evening
to the leaves which the scorching heats of
noon have withered, *ros in herbâ.* Thou art
fair as the orb of night, *pulchra ut luna;* and
it is thou who settest again in the right way
the feet of the wandering traveller; thou art
brilliant as the dawn, *aurora consurgens;* mild
and pure as the star of morn, *stella matutina;*
and it is thou who dost herald the rising of
the Sun of justice in our hearts.

O Mary, I fail in power to show forth thy
greatness and thy manifold claims to our love,
and it is a joy to me to sink back overpowered
by a glory so vast. But since I am speaking
in the congregation of thy children, who are
also my brethren, I will utter without fear
the thoughts of my heart in regard of thy
praise.

At thy name, O Mary, the heavens rejoice,
and earth sings for gladness of heart, while

hell shudders in impotent wrath. None can truly invoke thine aid and perish. The stately temples reared by mighty nations, the gold, the banners wrought by royal hands, and the humble thank-offerings laid by the mariner on the threshold of some lowly chapel, the homage of highest art and the rude image traced by martyr hands on some wall of the catacombs,—all alike attest thy power to still every storm that perils the heart of man, and to draw down on us the mercy of our God. Mary, I have seen the wildest spots of earth smile at thy name and put on gracefulness; the pious dwellers in the far-off wilderness sing thy glories; the echoing mountains and the ever-sounding torrents are vocal with thy praises. I have seen, in earth's most stately cities, the purest and noblest virtues flourish under the shadow of thy name; I have seen the thought of thee and the pure joy of thy feasts preferred to earth's most winning fascinations..... I have seen old men, after sixty, eighty years of a life void of faith and of virtue, rise on the bed of sickness; remember, at sound of thy name, the God who had crowned their infancy with blessings; and thou didst beam upon their dying eyes as a pledge of safety and of everlasting peace......
O Mary, who art thou, then? *Quæ est ista?* Thou art the Mother of our Saviour; and Jesus God over all, blessed for evermore, is the fruit of thy womb; thou art our sister, senor

nostra es ; daughter of Adam, thou hast no part in our fatal heritage, and our woes elicit thy deepest, tenderest commiseration.

O Mary, thou art the noblest creation of he power of God. Thou art the most winning device of His goodness. Thou art the sweetest smile of His mercy. O God, open the eyes of those who see not, that they may see Mary, and know the sweet radiance of her mother's eyes. Touch the hearts which love her not ; for to faith there is but one step from Mary to the Eternal Word, to that beauty ever old, yet ever new ; to that uncreated light which healeth our blinded eyes and satisfieth our largest desires, from Mary to Jesus, from the Mother to the Son.

Brother well-beloved,—and I am happy in being the first to greet you by this name,— you see under what favourable auspices you make your entry into this new Jerusalem, which is the dwelling-place of God,—into *the Church of the living God, which is the pillar and ground of the truth* ..... But before I allow your heart to expand to the fulness of joys which await it, there is a solemn lesson for you to-day ; and, as I am the first to cause you to hear the joyful sound of the Gospel, I dare not hide from you its most austere teaching. You have understood all, you tell us ; but permit me to ask you, have you understood the mystery of the cross ? ..... Take good heed —it is the basis and ground-work of Christianity.

MARIE-ALPHONSE RATISBONNE.   **63**

I do not mean now that hallowed cross
which you lovingly revere, because it brings
before you Jesus crucified in expiation of
your sins.   Let me borrow the energetic language of an ancient apologist of our faith, and
say to you : We are not now concerned with
the cross which it is so blessed to revere, but
of that cross which you must learn to bear.
Ecce cruces jam non adorandæ, sed subeundæ.
This is what you must thoroughly understand,
if you are a Christian ; and this is what your
baptism has already taught you. . . . . .

Moreover, it were vain to attempt to
conceal it, it can scarcely be that your future life should offer you no cross to be
borne.   I see them preparing; undoubtedly
you must revere them from afar, but there
is something better than that—you must accept them when they come near and endure
them with good courage.   I am greatly deceived if patience be not the appointed
means of increasing and strengthening your
faith, and enabling you to bring forth its
fruits.   And bless God for it.   You have
been brought within the Christian Church
by Mary and by the Cross.   It is an introduction of good augury.   Blessed be God
for it! for I know He has given you ears
to hear and a heart to understand this language.   Son of the Catholic Church, you
will share the destiny of your Mother!
Look out on Rome, the spot on which you

have just been new-born unto God! Continuous conflict and continuous triumph—this
is her earthly heritage; and thus nothing
appals by its novelty, after eighteen centuries of warfare and of victory......
  It is at the very centre of Catholic unity,
at the footstool of the highest apostolical
chair, whence flash forth the keenest purest
rays of the faith to pierce the darkness of
paganism, heresy, and judaism, that the
Church has poured on your brow the sav-
ing stream of regeneration. It is Peter himself, that Moses of the new law, worthily
represented by the first vicar of his illustrious successor, who has smitten for you
the rock of wonder, the immovable stone :
Petra erat Christus, whence flows that water which springeth up unto eternal life. It
is in the living flame of the Holy Ghost
that you have been baptised : *Spiritu Sancto
et igne*. The splendours of the noblest ceremonies of our religion fall full upon you,
and we who are round about you catch
some gleams of their glory. It is to-day
your Pentecost, and the Spirit of might and
of love hath filled your heart! It is to-day
your Paschal time, and Jesus Christ is about
to feed you with His sacred Flesh and with
His precious Blood. It is He Himself whom
you will receive, really, substantially, and
truly; your faith, your emotion, the tears
which stream from your eyes, anticipate all

I would say. Fear not that I shall weary you now with long and insipid exposition and proof of a truth which it is your high blessedness to believe. I will say but one word, which you will feel to be true,—Jesus Christ is far too truly our God and our friend that He should feed our souls with an empty figure, and cheat our love with a baseless illusion; besides, we need Him thus; for He commands us to love Him so as to be ready to lay down our lives for Him, and the Divine Eucharist has ever been the food and the strength of martyrs. Hear what Christian antiquity hath believed and hath handed down. . . . . .

But I pause, for I am retarding your blessedness. Now, at this moment, the eyes of heaven look lovingly down upon you, and earth gives you its added blessing, and Jesus Christ awaits you. Go forward, then—the angels of God have begun this glad rejoicing, and the children of God echo it along here in earth; and he who seemed to our eyes to die, and whose spirit liveth in the hands of the Lord, you know that his desires and his prayers have not been wanting—the solemn moment is come.

Abraham, Isaac, and Jacob, patriarchs and prophets cheer you on from out of heaven; and Moses gives you his blessing, because the law written in your heart hath met and recognised the Gospel; mercy and

6*

truth uphold you, justice and peace compass
you round about, repentance and innocence
crown you with gladness; and it is Mary
who receives you and who protects you.

O Mary, it is an imperious want of our
hearts, no less than a duty, to utter yet
once again the prayer to which we owe, it
may be, the consolations of this happy day.
And throughout this vast assembly, behold,
with one heart and one voice we say:

"Remember, O Mary, Virgin most piti-
ful, that it has never been heard from old
time that any one who has fled to thy protection, implored thine aid, and sought thine
intercesson, has been left desolate. Groan-
ing beneath the burden of our sins, we
come, O Virgin of virgins, to cast ourselves
into thine arms. O Mother of the Word,
remember now those who stand in grace,
those who are in sin; remember now those
who know thee, and those who know thee
not; remember now all our miseries, and
all thy tender pity. I will not say: Remember this youth; for he is thy child, and
the blessed and glorious conquest of thy
love; but I will say to thee: Remember
those friends so dear, for whom he offers
thee this day the first prayers of his Catholic heart; restore them to him in time, restore
them to him in eternity......

And since I am a stranger here,—but
no, there are no strangers at Rome—every

Catholic is a Roman,—but since we were
both born on the soil of France, I know
that I do but give utterance to the desires
of all hearts here present when I say to
thee : Remember France : it has still noble
virtues, generous souls, heroic self-devotedness. Bring back again upon the Church
of France the fair beauty of the days of old.

The holy sacrifice of the Mass closed the
ceremony. It was scarcely possible to witness without a quickening of faith, the fervour
with which the new convert prayed, and the
silent recollectedness with which all the congregation united their prayers to his. It was
especially at the solemn moment of communion that our Lord seemed to pour down
His sweetness and His graces upon the pious
multitude. Our dear brother Ratisbonne
was so annihilated by his consciousness of the
Divine Presence, that it was necessary to sup-
port him as he drew near to the holy table ;
and after having received the Bread of angels,
he was unable to rise without the aid of Father Villefort and of his sponsor. His tears
flowed abundantly ; he was quite overcome
by the depth and complexity of his emotions,
and by the ineffable graces with which our
Lord filled his soul.

To see this young man, but a few days
before an obstinate Jew, and now a Catholic

glowing with faith and charity, one could not help saying to one's self; O Lord, Thou art wonderful in all Thy works. And the profound exclamation of the convert was ever present to our thoughts: *I understood all.*

A large number of persons gave the young convert the truest proof of their brotherly love, by following him to the holy table. This pious communion in our Lord was most edifying, and gave to the whole ceremony a character of fervour and of love.

In this sacred banquet, in which the chosen friends of God celebrated the ever-new miracle of his mercy, every heart was joined in love to the family that was sorrowing beneath the visitation of God's hand. The thought of the beloved and venerable man whose departure from earth they mourned, threw a reflection of the heavenly glory over this pious solemnity. *O, how this gentleman has prayed for me!* were Ratisbonne's words, at the moment when the veil fell from his eyes, and when he knew nothing of this fervent Christian but that he had passed from earth. O Lord, I adore the depth of Thy councils. The prophet-king asked of old; Shall the dust of the tomb give thanks unto Thy name, and declare Thy truth? Yes, Lord, for Thou hast heard the prayer of the righteous man, and Thou hast poured down with full hands Thy consolations, into the wounds and sorrows of earth, that we may

learn to give glory to Thy name; and not allow ourselves to sink into despondency; *Ut
cantet tibi gloria mea, et non compunger.*

And now it was finished and done. Ratisbonne has been admitted to all the joys, to
all the graces of Catholic life. Blessed be
God who hath given us yet another brother;
the voice of joy and of thanksgiving is in the
dwellings of the just; the song of triumph
peals to the vault of the temple; the restrained emotion of every heart finds utterance. *Te Deum laudamus!* we praise Thee,
O God! shouted the congregation in one
ecstatic burst: we praise *Thee.* And then
we began to feel, with a thrill of joyful mirth,
what is the communion of saints. Those
manifold voices, mingled in one triumphal
shout of gratitude, gave us a foretaste of the
blessedness of heaven. The heart that could
remain cold and unmoved amidst the enthusiasm of this sublime shout was surely not the
heart of a Catholic.

After the *Te Deum,* the cardinal led the
new-born child of the Church into the house
of the Jesuits: and it is said, that when they
had left the sacred building, he could not
constrain his emotion, but pressed to his
heart with paternal tenderness him whose
feet he had set in the way of life.

Ratisbonne's joy was indescribable. Surrounded by a crowd of persons eager to see
him, to hear him, to embrace him, he received

the congratulations of all with a bounding
gladness of heart at being now a son of the
holy Catholic family.

An eye-witness relates, that when at length
he retired to the cell he had occupied during
his retreat, his first act was to prostrate himself before his crucifix, to thank the Saviour
of the world for the graces which had been
vouchsafed to him.

And as for those whose privilege it was to
be present at this glorious ceremony, they
went away with this consoling truth graven
on their inmost hearts: that when a man seeks
God sincerely, He soon cometh, even though
a miracle be needed to make plain His way
before Him.

When God, in His fatherly tenderness,
bestows on His children some of those extraordinary favours which rekindle faith and
flood the heart with a love passing all understanding, they feel as if they would make here
their tents amidst the delights of this interior
joy, and prolong and retain all that has con-
tributed to it—all that may perpetuate it.

In order to satisfy the pious desire of devout souls, we will linger yet awhile beside
the happy child of Mary; we will follow his
steps and listen to his words from the thrice-
blessed day when he was united to us by par-
taking of the holiest of mysteries, to the time
when this account is given to the world.

And he, too—he longed to abide on that Thabor. Object of such rare and abundant grace; having thrown far from him, like a garment worn out, the miseries of his past life; adorned in that baptismal innocence, which, alas, so soon contracts stain in the world, he pined for solitude, dreaded the throng of men, evaded the eager curiosity of all, and, as it were, set a seal upon his heart, lest any of the treasures confided to him by God should be lost.

He manifested, then, a great desire to pass in retreat the days of dissipation which were drawing near. With what eye would he gaze upon the fond pleasures and vain joys of earth; he, to whom it had been given to gaze upon the mystic Rose, upon that fairest Flower of Heaven, and who, in the fervour of his nascent faith, in the deep joy of his gratitude and love, was learning how sweet the Lord is!

But before entering upon this fresh retreat, which could be but an uninterrupted song of thanksgiving, there remained one duty to be discharged, one new happiness to be enjoyed. Having become the child of the Church, he yearned for the moment when he might be allowed to cast himself at the feet of the venerable Pontiff, who guides with so sure a hand, through the raging storm and wind, the bark which bears us all towards the heavenly haven.

We have heard the touching details o

this interview; and that we may make our
readers partakers of our joy, we must seek an
illustration from the most precious memories
of Catholicism.

Those who have visited the catacombs will
remember, that at every step they met the
image of the Good Shepherd bearing back to
the fold the wandering sheep; they will have
remarked the expression of satisfied love, of
fatherly tenderness, which the simple art of
the first ages has rendered so truly. Let them
now recall the feelings excited by this ever-
recurring image, and then they may form
some idea of this touching scene.

M. Ratisbonne and M. Théodore de Bussières were introduced to his Holiness by the
reverend father the General of the Company
of Jesus. After the customary genuflexions,
they received that mighty benediction which
Catholics prize so highly.

The holy Father conversed with them for
some time, and gave them many precious
tokens of his affection, with all the frank and
tender love of a father. He gave directions
that they should be taken to see the interior
of his palace. Pushing them before him,
with a gracious familiarity, he led them into
his bedchamber. Then the venerable successor of the Prince of the Apostles gave them a
touching evidence of his own trust in the
protection of her whom the Church invokes
as the Help of Christians; he showed them an

image of the blessed Virgin which he reveres
with an especial devotion, and which is placed
close to his bed.   And then, wishing that M.
Ratisbonne should preserve some memorial of
his visit, his Holiness gave him, with his own
hands, a crucifix to which special indulgences
were attached.

And if, when the days of trial and of conflict come, the new soldier of the faith shall
need to refresh his courage, let him remember the sacred standard which the visible
head of the Church then placed in his youthful hands; and, beholding his crucifix, let him
say confidently, *In hoc signo vinces.*

Perhaps M. Ratisbonne will leave us before he has time to take root in this land of
promise.   It is so delightful to see one's family after a long absence, to embrace a brother who has preceded one in the way of the
Lord.   Far from weakening the heart's true
ties, the Gospel sanctifies them and draws
them closer; its most faithful disciples will
ever be, in all that is not opposed to the law
of God, the most tender of sons, the most devoted of friends.

If, then, Providence remove him too soon
from our brotherly affection, let him go, like
another apostle, fresh from the upper chamber,
and manifest in his own country and in his
father's house his new virtues, and exert the

7

gentle constraint of his prayers, and diffuse
the fragance and the grace of his youthful
soul, which, born but yesterday into Catholic
life, is still adorned with all the charms of infancy.

The earliest longings, the first thoughts of
his heart, were for the regeneration of his
brethren. Well, the Lord has read his secret
heart, and has blessed him in regenerating
that heart. In whatever way it may please
God to lead him, our tender prayers will go
with him, to draw down upon him the grace
of perseverance; that the Author of every
good and perfect gift may endue him with
strength for the fight, with patience in the
trial, with humility in the flush of victory, and
a glowing charity.

Every young life is exposed to storm; hap-
pier than we are, he has been crowned before
the conflict; but the evil days will come.
May he then remember his brethren at Rome!
May he never forget Mary, his mother!

BAPTISM OF M. MARIE-ALPHONSE RATISBONNE.

Extract from the letter of an eye-witness.

Paris, February 2d, 1842.

A few weeks since a stranger arrived in
Rome. He was young and rich; he has all
the habits of that elegance, all the tastes of
that brilliant frivolity, which education and
fortune impart to young men of his age and
stamp. He asks nothing of Italy but to be
lulled by the soft languors of her winters, and
some rays of the sun of her antique glory, of
the deathless splendour of her sky and of her
summers, the ever-fresh charm of her old
memories, and the fragance of poetry which
exhales from her ruins, hallowed by great
deeds and by great men.... In the secret
heart of this young man there is one more serious thought, one profound and impetuous
energy of feeling; he is a Jew, and he views
Catholicism with all the prejudices and hatred
of his race—with a hatred at once keen, im-
placable, and *sombre;* he even avoids Rome
altogether. Still he has come thither, in his
own despite almost; but he has scarcely arrived
when he numbers the days for his departure.
He has witnessed the moral degradation of
his co-religionists, who are restrained to the

filthiest quarter of the city—he charges it on
the Catholics; and his hatred finds expression
in bitter sarcasms, in horrible blasphemies.
The very morning of the day fixed for his departure he wrote to his uncle : " I leave this
city with a profound horror, and curse it as I
go....." And that very day, a few hours
later, this same young man casually enters a
lonely church, falls on his knees overwhelmed
and annihilated, rises bathed in tears, and
asks for a Catholic priest, not to receive instruction, but to be baptised : his conversion
was accomplished—he had *understood all*.
What, then, had taken place in this church?
What has he seen? what has he heard? I
can tell you, for all Rome is vocal with it.
But these are things belonging to an order so
high and so holy, that it is the prerogative of
the Church alone to utter them with the in-
fallible warrant of her word. She will speak,
and you will soon know all. So far as I am
concerned, I will only relate to you to-day,
without one touch of exaggeration, the facts
of this conversion just as it happened, just as
it struck me. It would be in itself an inexplicable miracle, even if a miracle had not
been its efficient cause.

Mr. Alphonse Ratisbonne belongs to one
of the chief Jewish families of Strasburg.
Now, as if to accumulate moral impossibilities
in the way of his conversion, God has permitted that its result should be obviously the

ruin of his fairest hopes of fortune. and of the
deepest affections of his heart. It severs the
bonds of a love which has been already hallowed by solemn espousals. "A week since,"
he writes to his betrothed, "if any unforeseen
calamity had compelled me to give you up, I
could not have had the courage to do so; I
should have died in the effort..... Now, to-
day, if my new faith is to divide us, I shall
offer this sacrifice to God without shedding .
one tear; and all my life long I shall pray
that He may bless and enlighten you, and
grant that we may meet in heaven."

Alphonse Ratisbonne made his public
abjuration on the 31st of January, in the
church of the Gesù, in presence of Cardinal
Patrizi. The young catechumen, clothed in a
long robe of white silk, was placed at the bottom of the church, below the barrier which
separated him from the holy place, in compliance with the ancient custom preserved in
our ritual. I did not then know him; but an
undefinable interest, excited by the miraculous circumstances of his conversion, drew me
towards him. I got as near to him as I could,
rather to read upon his features the impressions of his soul, than to follow the touching
ceremony of his abjuration. The cardinal,
having prayed awhile at the altar, and as-
sumed his pontifical vestments, went in procession towards the catechumen, at the bottom
of the nave of the church. There commenced
7*

the ceremonies and exorcisms. Never had I
so felt the Divine character of that ritual, so
full of mysteries. Can you conceive any
thing more thrilling than this dialogue:
"What do you crave?"
"Baptism."
"What besides?"
"Life."
"Do you renounce the Devil?"
"I renounce him."
"Do you believe in Jesus Christ?"
"I do believe in him."
He, a descendant of those Jews who hanged
Him on the wood of shame? All that is
merely formal and outward had disappeared
here. That firm, brief, energetic speech;
that decided but modest look at the bishop
who is questioning him; the noble firmness
of his attitude, and the unruffled placidity of
his features, the paleness of which was relieved by the faintest flush,—all these indi-
cations of a resolute, thoughtful, and collected
character brought home to me the grandeur
of this conflict, in which the rarest and most
testing courage, that of a profound conviction
without enthusiasm, without an enthralling
imagination, had conquered that which is
mightiest and most tenacious of life in the
heart of man—his early faith and his first
love. A sigh of ineffable happiness escaped
from his breast ; a smile, like a ray of heav
enly beatitude, hovered around his lips, as

he raised his head, moist and dripping with
the waters of Baptism. It was clear—every
eye might see it—he had crossed a great
gulf; he breathed, he was a Christian.

And then every barrier of the Church fell
down before the innocence and the faith of
this regenerated soul. Amidst the benedictions of the enormous crowd that filled the
nave and just opened a pathway for him as
he passed, the young neophyte was led to
the altar. He there received the sacrament
of Confirmation at the hands of the cardinal.
As the gifts of the Holy Ghost descended, together with the blessing of the bishop, upon
his head, he seemed to me oppressed beneath
the torrent of grace ; the waves of gladness
that flowed in upon him were too vast—came
too suddenly, too impetuously. It seemed as
though, before opening his heart to the heavenly joys of his first communion, he needed
time and rest to control his excess of holy
emotion. The ceremony was suspended a
while   A voice, well known and dear to this
pious congregation,—almost all French, or
Catholic strangers, to whom the glorious pop-
ularity of our language was, like the faith, a
common bond,—was heard celebrating the infinite mercies of God, and the wondrous
patronage of Mary, manifested in the city of
Rome towards a son of France. The Abbé
Dupanloup's heart poured forth, spontane-
ously and without effort, a stream of lofty

.anguage, with the grace and masculine energy of a living faith, and with bursts of
pathetic eloquence, to which his congregation
could respond only by their tears.

At length the holy Sacrifice of the Mass
began. I could not remove my eyes from
M. Ratisbonne, absorbed entirely in his fulness of joy and in the fervour of his prayer.
I fancied I could read upon his soul the
growing impression of the bleeding memorials of Calvary. But I cannot express my
meaning. And how shall I speak of this new
pasch of this new Christian ? How convey to
you a notion of the solemn moment when the
cardinal, tremulous with emotion, placed the
sacred host upon his lips ? At this last, highest
grace, the vessel of election flowed over.
He who had been, up to this moment, so
calm in his fervour, so collected and firm, so
entirely master of his deep feelings, could
not now contain the fulness of this new and
unknown bliss ; he sobbed passionately, and
was led almost fainting from the altar to his
assigned place. And then was illustrated, in
its sweetest symbol, the Catholic dogma of
the communion of saints,—that mystery of
universal and brotherly oneness, in virtue of
which ten thousand times ten thousand of
every tongue and of every land, who know
not each other's names, meet and are one in the
mystic feast, breaking together the bread of
life everlasting, and drinking at one chalice

the wine of boundless infinite charity. Noble
ladies, girls in the first bloom of youth, young
men, and men whose names and whose deeds
are written .n their country's annals, drew
near with one accord to the holy table, offering
to God for the new convert their fervent com-
munions, just as mothers would have done for
their children, or sisters for a brother, or friend
for beloved friend.   And the people, moved by
this spectacle, joined their prayers and blessings by words, spoken loud—words of a
simple sweetness and charm which cannot be
transferred from their native Italian.   At
length the *Te. Deum* thundered forth,—no
other word can express the electrical effect of
that exulting shout of thanksgiving, blending
with the noble organ and the pealing bells of the
Gesù.   It is not a hymn of the Church, grave
and measured, but rather the living acclaim
of an enormous multitude swaying beneath
an overmastering religious enthusiasm.   I
pray God that the memory of what I felt during those three hours may never be effaced
from my heart; an impression like that is
undoubtedly one of the most precious boons
that can be bestowed upon a Christian soul.

OF

MARIE-ALPHONSE RATISBONNE

TO M. DUFRICHE-DESGENETTES,

Founder and Director of the "Archiconfrérie de Notre-Dame des Victoires," at Paris.

THIS letter was published in the first bulletin of the annals of the Archconfraternity. It was introduced by the curé of Notre-Dame des Victoires, with the following preface.

The news of the conversion of M. Alphonse Ratisbonne was communicated to the Arch-confraternity of the Sacred Heart of Mary on Sunday, January 30th, 1842, at the evening service. It was brought by his brother, M. l'Abbé Théodore Ratisbonne, our sub-director. It would be impossible to describe the impression produced on all present by this touching and interesting narrative. When the Abbé Ratisbonne, after having recounted the circumstances of this wonderful conversion added, " This Alphonse, of whom I am speaking to you, is my brother..." the emotion of the congregation became most intense, and a prolonged murmur of wonder and of joy was heard throughout it. They had been

marvelling at the Divine mercy, and rejoicing
in the return of this prodigal to his father's
house, with the common joy of Christians;
but at the words, " he is my brother," all the
congregation shared the rapture of the pious
ecclesiastic, all felt that they too had gained
a brother. At the request of many members
of our confraternity, we sang the *Magnificat* in
thanksgiving, just before I mounted the pul-
pit. For more than a year the family of the
young neophyte had been the object of our
eager desires and prayers, and, but a fortnight
before his conversion, Alphonse had been
again and specially commended by his brother
to our public prayers.

As I wished to diffuse throughout the whole
confraternity the sacred joy which filled our
own hearts, and as I was anxious that my account should be scrupulously exact, I begged
M. Marie-Alphonse Ratisbonne to be kind
enough to give me, himself, a statement of the
circumstances of his conversion; and I feel
great pleasure in publishing the following extract from the letter he wrote in reply :

College of Juilly, 12th *April,* 1842.

My first thought and the first instinct of
my heart, at the moment of my conversion,
was to bury myself and my secret in the cloister, so that I might find refuge from the world,
which could no longer understand me, and
give myself entirely to my God, who had gi-

ven me such a glimpse of the spiritual world.
I was reluctant to speak without the permission of a priest. He, who was to me the representative and voice of God, commanded
me to make known what had happened to
me; and I did so, in so far as words enabled
me to express my meaning. And now, after
some weeks of retirement and retreat, I will
try to set down a greater fulness of detail; and
it is fitting that sinners should give an account
of the graces vouchsafed to them to you, M. le
Curé—to you who have founded the Arch-
confraternity for the conversion of sinners.

If I had only to apprise you of the fact
of my conversion, one single, word would
suffice—the name of Mary. But your confraternity is eager to have a full account;
you wish to know who and what is this
son of Abraham, who has found at Rome
life, and grace, and happiness. I will, there-
fore, first invoke the aid of my heavenly
Mother, and then set before you, in very
simple words, the course and order of my
life.

My family is known well enough, for its
members are rich and generous; and it has
long occupied a high station in Alsace. It
is said that my ancestors have been very
godly men; Christians as well as Jews have
blessed the name of my grandfather, the
only Jew who obtained, under Louis XVI.,
not only the right to hold property at Stras-

burg, but a patent of nobility. Such was
my family; but now all traditions of religion are effaced from it.

I began my studies at the Royal College
of Strasburg, where I made far greater progress in the depravation of my heart than
in the education of my mind.

It was in the year 1825 (I was born May
1st, 1814) that an unexpected event inflicted
a heavy blow on my family. My brother
Theodore, of whom the highest hopes were
entertained, avowed himself a Christian; and
soon after, nowithstanding the grief he had
occasioned and the earnest entreaties of our
parents, he became a priest, and exercised
his ministry in the same city, and before
the very eyes of my disconsolate family.
Young as I was, my brother's conduct
shocked me greatly, and I conceived a violent
hatred of his office, and of his person and
character. Brought up amongst young Christians, who were quite as reckless and indifferent as I was myself, I had not, up to
that time, felt either sympathy or antipathy
towards Christianity; but my brother's conversion, which I looked upon as an act of
unaccountable folly, made me believe all I
heard of the fanaticism of the Catholics, and
I held them accordingly in great horror.

I was about this time, withdrawn from
college to be placed in a Protestant institution, the magniloquent prospectus of which
8

had dazzled my parents. The younger members of the great Protestant families of Alsace and of Germany came there, to be moulded upon the fashionable life of Paris, and abandoned themselves to pleasures of all kinds, far more than to study. Nevertheless, I presented myself for examination when I left this institution, and, by a piece of good luck I little deserved, I was admitted Bachelor of Arts.

I was then sole master of my patrimony; for my mother had died while I was still young, and my father had survived her but a few years. But I had a worthy uncle, the patriarch of the family, a second father to me, who, having no children of his own, had centred all his affection in those of his brother.

This uncle, so well known in the financial world for his lofty integrity as well as for his extraordinary capacity, wished much to give me a share in the bank of which he is the head; but I first of all read law at Paris, and, after having obtained the diploma of a licentiate and put on my advocate's gown, I was recalled to Strasburg by my uncle, who exerted all his influence to settle me with himself. I cannot number all his cares and kindnesses : horses, carriages, pleasant travels, a thousand acts of lavish affection, were mine, and he had not the heart to refuse me any thing. My uncle gave me a more positive mark of his confidence still : he gave me the signature of the bank, and he promised me besides the title and the solid advantages of a partner—a promise which he carried into effect the first of January in this year, 1842. I was at Rome when this information reached me.

My uncle had only one matter of complaint —my frequent journeys to Paris. You are too fond of the *Champs-Élysées*, said he affectionately to me. He was right. I loved nothing but pleasures; business annoyed me, the atmosphere of the office stifled me; I had a notion that people came into the world simply to enjoy themselves; and, although a kind of natural and instinctive modesty kept me from baser pleasures and associates, I thought of nothing but fêtes and rejoicings, and gave myself up to them with passionate ardour.

It was fortunate that about this time a good work offered itself to my eager need of action, and I threw myself into it with all my heart. It was the work of the *regeneration* of the poor Israelites, as it was erroneously called; for I have now learned that something more than money and lotteries of charity is requisite to regenerate a people destitute of religion. But I honestly believed in the possibility of this renovation, and I became one of the most zealous members of the Society for the providing occupation for young Jews, —a society which my brother had founded at Strasburg fifteen years before, and which has lasted until now, notwithstanding its limited resources. I managed to fill its coffers, and fancied I had done something very great.

O Christian charity, how thou wouldst smile at my lofty self-satisfaction! The Jew thinks a great deal of himself when he has given a great deal; the Christian gives all and despises himself—he despises himself until he has given himself in addition; and when he has sacrified himself whole and entire, he despises himself still.

Although I had no religion whatever, I was busy with the worldly condition of my *co-religionists.* I was a Jew by profession. and that is all; for I did not even believe in God. I never opened a religious book; and neither in my uncle's house nor in those of my brothers and sisters was there the slightest observance of the injunctions of Judaism.

There was a fearful void in my heart, and I was not happy, though I possessed every thing in abundance, in profusion. Something was still lacking; and this something I found, at least so I fondly fancied; and it was thus:

I had a niece, the daughter of my eldest brother, who had been destined to me from our childhood. She was growing up, under my own eyes, in beauty and in gracefulness, and in her I beheld the fair promise of my future life, and the satisfaction of all my hopes. I do not think it seemly to set forth here the praises of her who was my betrothed. It

would be useless to those who do not know
her; but those who have seen her know that
it would not be easy to imagine a young girl
more gentle, more amiable, more charming.
She was to me a creature apart, who seemed
formed expressly to complete my existence;
and when the desires of all our family, combined with our mutual symathy and affection,
fixed the time of my long-wished-for marriage,
I thought that nothing could be thenceforth
wanting to my happiness.

And thus, after the ceremony of our be
trothal, I had the pleasure of seeing all
my family overflowing with joy, and my
sisters so happy! They had but one reproach to make—I loved my bride too exclusively, and they confessed their jealousy; for
I may say in passing, that there are few
families so happy as mine: the most intimate and perfect union of hearts, the most
tender affection, reigns amongst my brothers
and sisters—an affection which verged on
idolatry. . . . And, indeed, my sisters are so
good, so loving, and so lovely. . . . Why, alas,
are they not Christians?

There was only one member of our family
who was hateful to me—my brother Theodore. And yet he loved us well; but his
soutane repelled me, his presence oppressed me
with gloom, his grave and serious conversation
excited my wrath. About a year before my
betrothal I had found it impossible to restrain
q*

my feelings, and I expressed them to him in a letter, which was intended to sever all connection between us for ever. The occasion was this. A child was lying in the agony of death ; my brother Theodore had the assurance to ask permission to baptise it, and he would probably have succeeded, if I had not been informed of his intention. I looked on it as an unworthy and dishonourable attempt ; I wrote to the *priest* to try his strength with men and not with children ; and I accompanied these words with so many invectives and threatenings, that I am even now astonished that my brother did not answer me a single word. He continued his relations with the rest of the family ; but I would never see him again, and I cherished a blind and bitter hatred against priests, and churches, and convents, and especially against the Jesuits, whose very name goaded me to frenzy.

Fortunately my brother left Strasburg, and so gratified my most earnest wish. He was summoned to Paris, to Notre Dame des Victoires, where, he said as he bade us farewell, he should not cease to pray for the conversion of his brothers and sisters. His departure relieved me of a heavy weight ; I even yielded so far to the entreaties of my family as to write him a few words of apology on the occasion of my betrothal. He answered my letter affectionately, and commended to my care some few poor people in whom he felt interested; and I gave them some trifling sum.

After this sort of reconciliation I had no further connection with Theodore, and I had altogether ceased to think of him; I had forgotten him quite. . . and he, the while, was praying for me!

I ought to mention here a kind of revolution in my religious notions which took place about the time of the ceremony of my betrothal. As I have said, I believed in nothing; and in this complete nullity, this negation of all faith, I found myself perfectly in harmony with my young friends, whether Catholic or Protestant. But the look of my bride awakened within me a mysterious sense of human dignity and worth; I began to believe in the immortality of the soul; more than that, I began, by a kind of instinct, to pray to God; I thanked Him for my happiness: and for all that I was not happy. . . I could not analyse and account for my feelings; I looked on my sweet bride as my good angel; I often told her so; and, indeed, the thought of her raised my heart towards a God whom I knew not, whom I had never before invoked.

It was deemed right, by reason of the tender age of my bride, to postpone our marriage. She was only sixteen years old. I was to undertake a voyage of pleasure to beguile the time of expectation. I scarcely

knew whither to direct my wanderings; one
of my sisters, who is settled in Paris, wished
me to remain with her; a dear friend wanted
to take me off to Spain. I declined the invitations of some others, who made me very
attractive propositions. I resolved, at length,
to go straight to Naples, to pass the winter at
Malta for the benefit of my rather delicate
health, and then to return home by way of the
East. I got letters of introduction for Constantinople even; and I set out about the end of
November, 1841, intending to return in the
spring of 1842.

My leave-taking was very melancholy. I
left behind me my beloved bride, an uncle
whose whole affection rested on me, sisters,
brothers, nieces, whose society was my most
valued delight; I left also those industrial
schools, those poor Jews with whom I was so
actively employed, and the numerous friends
who loved me—friends of my childhood,
whom I could not leave without shedding
tears; for indeed I loved them, and love them
still. . . .

To set out alone on so long a voyage! the
mere thought threw me into a state of profound sadness. But, said I to myself, perhaps God will send me some friend on my
way!

I recollect two singular incidents which
marked the days preceding my departure,
and which now strike me forcibly. I wished

belore leaving, to affix my signature to a
large number of receipts connected with the
subscriptions to the Jewish industrial society
. . . . . I dated them in advance January
15th, and by dint of writing this date so many
times, I became weary of it, and said, as I
laid down my pen:

"God only knows where I shall be on the
15th of January, and whether that day may
not be the day of my death."

On that day I arrived at Rome, and I regard it as the first dawn of my new life.

Another circumstance that interested me
was the meeting of several distinguished
Jews to consider the means of reforming the
worship of Judaism, and bringing it more
into harmony with the spirit of the age. I
went to the meeting, at which every one gave
his opinion on the improvements that were
suggested. There were as many opinions as
persons; there was a great deal of discussion;
they took into account the convenience of
man, the events of the times, the axioms of
public opinion, all the ideas of modern civili-
sation: every thing was thought of and
pondered, one only was forgotten—the law of
God. That did not seem to come into the
question at all; I cannot remember that the
name of God was mentioned once, or that of
Moses, or the existence of the Bible.

My own private opinion was, that they
should allow all religious forms to die quietly

out ; that they need not have recourse either
to books or to men, but that every one should
be left free to express and practise his faith
in his own fashion. This opinion proves my
lofty wisdom in matters of religion. I had
made progress as you will see. The meeting
broke up without coming to any decision.

But a Jew, more sensible than I, had
given utterance to a sentiment so remarkable,
that I will give it word for word : " We must
make haste to abandon this old temple, whose
crumbling walls are parting on all sides, unless we wish to be buried beneath its ruins ;"
words full of truth, words which every Jew
of our times murmurs to himself alone. But,
alas, eighteen centuries have passed since
they abandoned their ancient temple, and
they will not enter that new temple whose
gates are open to them by day and by night!

At length I set out. As I left Strasburg
I shed many tears ; I was disquieted by a
crowd of fears, by a thousand strange presentiments. When we stopped to change
horses, I was roused from my reverie by cries
of joy and the sound of music. It was a rustic
wedding—the happy, noisy villagers were just
issuing from the church—flutes and fiddles
were going vigorously ; the crowd came round
my carriage, as though to invite me to share
their joy. " It will be my turn soon," I exclaimed. And this thought restored my cheer-
fulness.

I spent some days at Marseilles. where
my friends and relatives received me with
open arms. I could scarcely tear myself
from all this elegant hospitality. And truly
it needs an effort to leave France, when one
leaves also a whole life of love, and of loving
memories and associations. Besides the ties
which bound me to her shores, the sea itself
seemed to oppose my departure; it rolled
along its mighty waves to bar my progress;
but all these obstacles were swept away by
the steamer which took me to Naples. I was
soon able to enjoy the magnificent type of
infinity above me and around me; but what
struck me more than sea or sky was *man*,
that frail creature who braves all dangers,
and masters the elements themselves. My
pride was loftier than the rolling waves,
more tenacious of its aims, and far less
easily subjugated.

The boat touched at Civita Vecchia on its
way to Naples. As we entered the harbour
the sound of cannon greeted our ears. I asked,
with a spiteful curiosity, the motive of this
warlike sound on the peaceful territory of the
Pope. I received for answer, " It is the feast
of the Conception of Mary." I shrugged my
shoulders and would not land.

The next day we reached Naples. The
sun was shining gloriously, and producing
brilliant effects on the smoke of Vesuvius.
Never had I been so dazzled by any scene of

nature. I saw before me the reality of those
glowing images of the heavens and the sea
with which artists and poets had stored my
fancy.

I passed a month at Naples, that I might
see and describe every thing. I wrote bitter
things against the religion and the priests,
who seemed to me so out of keeping with that
magnificent country. Oh, with what blasphemies did I fill my journal! And if I speak
of them now, it is that you may see how dark
and evil was my soul then. I wrote to Strasburg that I had drunk some *lachryma Christi*
on Vesuvius to the health of the abbé Ratisbonne, and that tears like that did me good
too. I cannot transcribe the horrible witticisms that I permitted myself to write.

My betrothed asked me if I agreed with
those who said : " See Naples and die." No,
I replied ; but see Naples and live ; live to see
it again. Such was my state of mind.

I had no wish to go to Rome, although
two friends of my family, whom I saw frequently, urged me strongly to do so ; I mean
M. Coulman, a Protestant, and formerly *dé-
puté* of Strasburg, and Baron Rothschild,
whose family lavished on me every kind of
attention and of gratification. I could not
yield to their persuasions..... My betrothed
wished me to go direct to Malta ; and she sent
me a recommendation from my physician that
I should spend the winter there, and carefully

avoid Rome, because of the malignant fevers which, he said, prevailed there.

These reasons would have prevented my going to Rome, even if I had placed this journey on my original programme. I thought I might possibly go there on my return, and I took my place in the *Mongibello* for Sicily. A friend accompanied me on board of the vessel, and promised to return and bid me farewell before we started. He came, but did not find me. If M. de Rèchecourt should ever learn the reason of my breach of engagement, he will be able to account for my apparent incivility, and will, I am sure, forgive me.

M. Coulman had introduced me to an amiable and estimable man who was going to Malta. I was so pleased at this, that I said to myself: "This is surely the friend God has sent me."

However, the first day of the new year arrived, and the vessel had not left. It was a sad day to me. I was alone at Naples; no one to congratulate me and wish me well, no one to press to my heart. I thought of my family, of the festivity and joy with which my uncle always kept that day; I began to shed tears, and the lively gaiety of the Neapolitans deepened my sadness. I went out, to shake off my importunate melancholy, and followed mechanically in the train of the crowd. I reached the *place* in front of the

6

palace, and found myself, I know not how, at
the door of a church. I went in. I think a
priest was saying Mass. I remained there,
leaning against a pillar, and my heart seemed
to open and expand in a new atmosphere. I
prayed after my own fashion, without taking
any notice of what was going on around me;
I prayed for my betrothed, for my uncle,
for my deceased father, for the loving mother who had been taken from me so early,
for all who were dear to me; and I asked of
God some inspiration, some intimation of His
will which might guide me in my projects
for improving the condition of the Jews,—
projects which haunted me incessantly.

My sadness passed away, like a cloud
which the wind breaks up and disperses; and
my heart was filled with an unutterable calmness, with a consolation such as I should have
felt if a voice had said to me : " Your prayer
is heard." Yes, it was heard,—heard far
beyond all expectation; for on the last day
of that same month I was to be baptised in
a church at Rome!

But how did I get to Rome?

I do not know, nor can I account for it in
any way. I almost fancy I must have missed
my way; for instead of going to the *bureau* of the Palermo boats, as I intended when
I left my lodging, I found myself in that of
the diligences for Rome. I told M. Vigne,
the friend who was to accompany me to

Malta, that I could not resist the temptation of making a short expedition to Rome, but that I would certainly be at Naples so as to leave with him on the 20th of January. I was wrong to pledge myself thus; for God disposes; and that 20th of January was destined to mark a very different crisis in my life. I left Naples on the 5th, and reached Rome on the 6th, the feast of the Epiphany. I had for my fellow-traveller an Englishman, named Marshall, whose original conversation amused me much.

Rome did not at first produce on me the impression I had expected. And I was so pressed for time, that I eagerly devoured ruins, ancient and modern, with the avidity of a thorough tourist. I filled my imagination and my journal with a confused medley of reminiscences. I visited with a monotonous admiration galleries, churches, catacombs, and all the innumerable magnificences of Rome. I was most frequently accompanied by my English friend, and by a *valet de place;* I have no notion what religion they were of, for neither of them gave any sign of Christianity in the churches, and I believed I behaved far more reverently than they did.

On the 8th of January, as I was going my round of sight-seeing, I heard some one calling me in the street; it was my old friend Gustave de Bussières. I was very happy to meet him, for my isolation had become pain-

ful to me. We went to dine with my friend's
father; and in that agreeable circle I felt some
measure of the joy with which one greets any
memorial of one's own country in a strange
land.

As I entered the drawing-room, M. Théodore de Bussières, the eldest son of this honourable family, was leaving it. I did not
know him personally, but I knew that he was
my brother's friend and namesake; I knew
that he had deserted Protestantism and become a Catholic, and this was quite enough
to inspire me with a profound antipathy to
him. I fancied that this feeling was recipro-
cal. However, as M. Théodore de Bussières
was already well known by his published volume of travels in Sicily and in the East, 1
was very glad to ask him some questions before starting on the same track; and whether
on this account, or from mere civility, I signi-
fied my intention of paying him a visit. He
answered me very kindly, and added, that he
had just received a letter from my brother the
abbé, and that he would give me his new address. " I will gladly receive it," said I, " although I shall not need it."

There our conversation ended; and when
he had left, I felt annoyed at the obligation 1
had imposed on myself to make a useless visit
and waste my very precious time.

I continued running about Rome all day
long except two hours in the morning which

I spent with Gustave; and in the evening I took my ease, either at the theatre or at some party. My conversations with Gustave were very animated; for the intercourse of two old schoolfellows furnishes inexhaustible store of amusing and interesting souvenirs. But he was a Protestant, with all the zeal and enthusiasm of the pietists of Alsace. He talked largely of the superiority of his sect to all other Christian communities, and was very eager to convert me; and I was much amused, as I had fancied that the mania of proselytism was peculiar to Catholics. I generally evaded his assaults by some merry jest; but once, to console him for the failure of his attempts, I promised him, that if ever I took it into my head to be converted, I would turn pietist; and he, on his part, promised that he would be present at my marriage, in the August following. All his efforts to detain me at Rome were ineffectual. Others of my friends, M. Edmund Humann and Alfred de Lotzbeck, joined with him in begging me to remain in Rome for the Carnival. But I could not consent; I feared I should grieve and distress my betrothed, and M. Vigne expected me at Naples in time to start with him on the 20th of January.

I was making the best use of the short time that remained, and went to the Capitol to visit the church of Aracœli. The impos-

9*

ing appearance of this church, the solemn chants which were echoing along its vast nave, the historical recollections awakened in me by the very soil I was treading,—all combined to produce a profound impression upon me. I was moved, penetrated, transported; and my *valet de place*, noticing my emotion, told me that he had frequently seen strangers affected in a similar way in that church.

As we came down from the Capitol, my *cicerone* led me through the Ghetto, the quarter assigned to the Jews. There I felt an emotion of an entirely different kind—mingled pity and indignation. What, I exclaimed, as I beheld that miserable sight, is this that Roman charity of which so much is said? I shuddered with horror, and I asked myself whether a whole nation deserved to be the victims of such barbarous treatment and of such endless prejudices, simply for having killed one man eighteen hundred years ago! Alas, I knew not then who this *One Man* was—I knew not the cry of blood which this people had uttered —a cry which I dare not repeat here, and which I cannot bear to recall. Rather would I dwell upon that other cry, wafted to heaven from the cross, *Father, forgive them; for they know not what they do!*

I described all that I had seen and felt to my family. I remember having written,

that I preferred being of the number of the
oppressed to being in the camp of the oppressors. I went back again to the Capitol,
and found the church of Aracœli in a great
bustle of preparation for some grand ceremony. I asked the object of it, and was
told that two Jews, named Constantini, of
A icona, were going to be baptised. I cannot describe the indignation I felt on re-
ceiving this information; and when my guide
asked me if I should like to be present I
exclaimed: " What! *I* assist at so infamous
a spectacle! No, no; I should not be able
to restrain myself from making a desperate
onslaught on both priests and victims."

I may say, without exaggeration, that I
never felt so fierce a hatred towards Christianity as after that visit to the Ghetto.
The stream of my mockery and blasphemy
flowed incessantly and inexhaustibly.

However, I had a few farewell visits to
make, and my promise to Baron de Bussières occurred to me continually as an
awkward obligation gratuitously taken on
myself. Most fortunately I had not asked
his address, and I resolved to make this
circumstance my excuse for not performing
my promise.

It was now the 15th, and I went to take
my place for Naples; my departure was
fixed for the 17th, at three A.M. I had two
days left, and I employed them, as usual,

in running about. But, as I was coming
out of a book-shop in' which I had been
looking over some works on Constantinople,
I met a servant of M. de Bussières senior,
on the *Corso*. He saluted me in passing,
and I stopped him to ask the address of
M. Théodore de Bussières : he replied, with
an Alsatian accent : Piazza Nicosia, No. 38.

And now, whether I liked it or not, I was
committed to this visit. I put it off to the
last moment, and at length set off, carrying
in my hand a card on which I had written *p.*
ρ. c. I found out this Piazza Nicosia, after
a great many turns and windings, and at
'ength reached No. 38. It was the very next
door to the bureau at which I had taken my
place for Naples the same day. I had made
a good round to reach the point from which
I had started—type of many a journey of
life on earth ! But from that point I set forth
on a journey of which I little thought !

My reception at the house of M. de Bussières was annoying. Instead of simply
taking my card, the servant suddenly an-
nounced me, and introduced me into the
drawing-room. I concealed my vexation as
well as I could beneath a civil smile, and I
took a chair near Madame de Bussières, who
was sitting with her two daughters, graceful
and gentle as the angels that Raphael painted.
Our conversation was at first very general
and unmeaning ; but it soon began to take the

tone and hue of the deep passion with which
I related my impressions of Rome.

I looked on M. de Bussières as a *dévot*, in
the illnatured sense of the word, and I was
very glad to have the opportunity of teasing
him about the Jews of Rome. It was a re-
lief to me to do so; but my complaints of
course led our conversation upon religious
ground. M. de Bussières spoke to me of the
majesty and grandeur of Catholicism; and I
replied with irony, and some of the many
imputations I had either heard or read; but
I could not help checking my impious frenzy,
out of respect for Madame de Bussières and
the two dear children who were playing at
her side. "Well," said M. de Bussières,
"since you detest superstition, and profess
yourself so very liberal in point of doctrine
—since you are so enlightened an *esprit fort*
—have you the courage to submit yourself
to a very simple and innocent test?"

"What test?"

"Only to wear a little something I will
give you; look, it is a medal of the Blessed
Virgin. It seems very ridiculous, does it
not? But, I assure you, I attach great value
and efficacy to this little medal."

This proposal, I confess, astonished me by
its puerile oddity. I did not expect such a
bathos. My first impulse was to laugh and
shrug my shoulders; but it struck me that
this scene could furnish me a delicious chap-

ter for my journal; and I consented to take the medal, that I might give it to my betrothed as a confirmation of my story. No sooner said than done. The medal was passed round my neck, not without difficulty, however, for the ribbon was rather too short. At length we succeeded ; I had the medal on my heart, and I exclaimed with a hearty laugh, " Ha, ha, here I am, a Catholic, apos· tolic and Roman!"

It was the devil prophesying by my mouth.

M. de Bussières felt a childlike pleasure in his victory, and was eager to grasp all its advantages. " Now," said he, " you must perfect the test; you must say every night and morning the *Memorare*, a very short and very efficacious prayer which S. Bernard addressed to the Blessed Virgin Mary."

" What do you mean, with your *Memorare ?*" I exclaimed ; "come, let us have done with this folly."

The name of S. Bernard reminded me of my brother, who had written the life of this great saint. I had never read his book ; and this association kindled afresh all my antipathy to proselytism, Jesuitism, and all those whom I called hypocrites and apostates.

I begged M. de Bussières to drop the subject; and I said, with a smile of contempt, that I regretted my not having a Hebrew prayer to offer him in return : but I had not one, and could not recollect one.

However, he persisted ; he said that by refusing to recite this short prayer I made the test useless, and that I proved thereby the reality of the wilful obstinacy with which the Jews were reproached. I did not wish to attach too much importance to the matter, and so I said : " Well, then, I promise you to say this prayer. Anyhow, if it does me no good, it cannot do me any harm." And M. de Bussières went to look for it, and gave it to me, begging me to copy it for him. I consented, on condition that I might keep the original, and give him my copy. I had no other thought than to enrich my journal with this additional *pièce justificative.*

And now we were both satisfied. Our conversation seemed to me whimsical and very amusing. I took my departure, and spent the evening at the theatre, thinking no more either of my medal or of the *Memorare.* But when I came home I found a note from M. de Bussières, who had called to return my visit, begging me to see him once more before I left Rome. I had to return his *Memorare ;* and as I was to leave in the morning, I packed my trunks and made all my preparations, and then I sat down and copied the prayer, *Memorare, O piissima Virgo.* . . . I wrote these words of S. Bernard mechanically, without thinking of their meaning. I was

very tired; it was very late, and I needed rest.

The next day, the 16th of January, I got my passport signed, and completed all my preparations ; but as I walked along I could not help repeating the words of the *Memorare.* Whence was it, O my God, that these words had taken so firm, so deep hold on my mind? I could not put them away ; they returned importunately upon me. I said them over and over again, just as one hums a tune which haunts one involuntarily and without conscious effort.

About eleven o'clock I called on M. de Bassières, to return to him his tenacious and peremptory prayer. I talked to him about my proposed travels in the East, and he gave me much excellent advice. "But," said he suddenly, "it is strange that you persist in leaving Rome at the very time when people are coming from all parts for the great ceremonies at St. Peter's. Perhaps you may never have the chance again ; and you will be sorry to have lost an opportunity which so many seek with eager curiosity."

I replied that my place was taken and paid for; that I had written to inform my family of my departure ; that I expected letters at Palermo; that it was now too late to think of changing my plans, and that my mind was made up. Our conversation was interrupted by the postman, who brought a letter from my brother, the Abbé Ratisbonne. He showed me the letter; but it was quite devoid of interest to me, as it related to a work which M. de Bussières was publishing in Paris. My brother did not even know that I was in Rome; but this unexpected episode threatened to close my visit, as I was eager to avoid every thing that could remind me of my brother.

Nevertheless, I was induced, by some incomprehensible influence, to prolong my stay at Rome. I granted to the urgency of a man whom I scarcely knew, what I had obstinately refused to my most intimate friends and companions.

And what, O my God, what was that irresistible impulse which led me to do what I had so firmly resolved not to do? Was it not a continuation of the same sweet force which brought me from Strasburg to Italy, notwithstanding my tempting invitations to Paris and to Valencia?—which led me from Naples to Rome, in spite of my firm determination to go straight to Sicily?—which at Rome compelled me, on the eve of my departure, to pay a visit which annoyed me, while I neglected others which I should have liked? O wonderful leadings of Providence? There is a mysterious influence which goes with us all along the course of our life. I had received the name of Tobias together with that of Alphonse. I had quite forgotten my

10

name ; but the unseen angel had not forgotten
me ; he was the true and helpful friend
whom God had sent me—but I knew him not
Alas, how many are there in the world who
know not the celestial guide of their journey
and who resist his gentle voice !

I had no wish to spend the Carnival in
Rome, but I did wish to see the Pope; and
M. de Bussières had assured me that I
should see him very soon at St. Peter's.
We took several rambles together. We
talked over every thing we saw—monuments, pictures, manners and customs ; but
religion contrived to mix itself with every
thing. M. de Bussières introduced it with
such charming simplicity, enforced it with so
keen and ardent a zeal, that I often said to
myself, that if any thing could disgust a man
with religion, it was the very importunity
with which his conversion was sought. My
natural gaiety led me to turn the most serious
subjects into ridicule, and the light flashes of
my fancy too often deepened into the fiendish
glare of blasphemy. Even now I shudder at
thought of those days.

And yet M. de Bussières was uniformly
calm and indulgent, even though he could not
conceal his grief. He even said once : " In
spite of your rage, I have a sure conviction
that you will be a Christian one day ; for there
is in you a groundwork of rectitude which
comforts me when I think of you, and per-

suades me that you will be enlightened, even though an angel from heaven be needed for that end."

"Ha, well and good," said I; "for else the matter would not be easy to manage."

As we passed the *Scala Santa*, M. de Buss.ères was seized with'a fit of enthusiasm. He rose up in the carriage, uncovered his head, and said in a tone of fervour: "Hail, *Scala Santa!* here is a sinner who will one day mount you on his knees!"

It would be utterly impossible to express the effect produced on me by this unexpected movement, this extraordinary honour paid to some old steps. I laughed at it as at something hopelessly, grotesquely mad; and as, a short time after, we drove through the charming gardens of the Villa Wolkonski, I rose and parodied his apostrophe by saying: "Hail, true marvels of God's power! It is before you that I kneel in homage, and not before an old staircase!"

These drives were repeated on the two following days, and lasted about two hours each. On the 19th, I saw M. de Bussières again, but he seemed sad and dejected. I withdrew from a motive of delicacy, without inquiring the cause of his sadness. Indeed, I did not learn this until the next day at noon, in the church of S. Andrea delle Fratte.

I was to leave on the 22d of January; for i had a second time taken my place for Na-

ples. The engagements of M. de Bussières
seemed to have diminished his zeal for my
conversion, and I fancied he had forgotten all
about his miraculous medal; but still I kept
on muttering to myself, though with an in-
conceivable impatience, that everlasting importunate invocation of St. Bernard.

In the middle of the night before the 20th
of January, I awoke suddenly, and saw before
me a large black cross, of a peculiar form,
and without the figure of our Lord. I made
many attempts to get rid of this image, but I
could not succeed; however I turned, there it
was always before me. I cannot say how
long this lasted, for I fell asleep at length;
and when I awoke in the morning I thought
no more of it.

I had to write several letters, and I remember that one of them, written to the
younger sister of my betrothed, ended with
the words, "*que Dieu vous garde*,"—may God
protect you! Some little time after I received
a letter from my bride, dated that same 20th
of January, and ending with the same words,
"*que Dieu vous garde!*" And, indeed, that
day was under the especial care and guar-
dianship of God.

Yet, if any one had said to me that morning, "You have risen a Jew; you will lie
down a Christian, . . ." I should have looked
on him as hopelessly, ludicrously mad.

This Thursday, January 20th, after having

taken breakfast at my hotel, and carried my letters to the post, I went to call on my friend Gustave, the pietist, who had just returned from a shooting excursion which had taken him for some days from Rome. He was surprised to see me still in Rome; I told him my motive for remaining was to see the Pope. "But I shall leave without seeing him after all, I said; for he took no part in the ceremony of the *Cathedra Petri*, although I had been led to hope he would do so."

Gustave consoled me ironically by speaking of another ceremony, and a very curious one, he said, which was to take place, I think, at S. Maria Maggiore. He alluded to the blessing of the animals; and thereupon followed a shower of jests and sarcasms, just such as you can imagine a Jew and a Protestant would utter.

We parted about eleven o'clock, after making an appointment for the next day to see a picture which had been painted for our countryman, Baron de Lotzbeck. I went off to a *café* in the Piazza di Spagna to look at the newspapers; and I had scarcely entered it when M. Edmond Humann sat down at my side, and we talked very gaily about Paris, and the fine arts and politics. Soon another friend accosted me; he was a Protestant, M. Alfred de Lotzbeck, with whom I held a conversation more frivolous still. We talked of hunting, of all kinds of pleasures, of the

10*

mir⌐h of the Carnival, of the brilliant *soirée*
given the evening before by the Duke de Tor-
lonia. Nor did we forget the fêtes of my ap-
proaching marriage, to which I invited M. de
Lotzbeck, who promised faithfully to be pre-
tent.

If at that moment—it was noon—a third
person had come up to me, and had said,
" Alphonse, in a quarter of an hour you will
be adoring Jesus Christ, your God and your
Saviour; you will be prostrate in a poor
church; you will be smiting your breast at
the feet of a priest in a convent of Jesuits,
where you will spend the Carnival in preparing for your baptism; and you will feel ready
to offer yourself in sacrifice for the Catholic
faith; you will renounce the world, its pomps,
its pleasures; your fortune, your hopes, your
bright glad future; and if necessary, you will
renounce your betrothed also, and the love of
your family, the esteem of your friends, the
attachment of the Jews;... and you will
have but one aspiration, to follow Jesus
Christ, and to bear His cross even unto
death;..."—I say that if some prophet had
uttered before me a prediction like this, I
should have thought that there could be only
one man more mad than he, the man who
could believe in the possibility of any thing
so absurd. And yet it is this absurdity and
folly which compose now my wisdom and **my**
happiness.

As I left the *café*, I met the carriage of
M. Théodore de Bussières. He stopped, and
asked me to go with him for a drive. The
weather was magnificent, and I accepted his
invitation with pleasure. But M. de Bussières asked my permission to stop a few minutes at the church of S. Andrea delle Fratte,
which was close by, as he had some little
business there. He asked me to wait for him
in the carriage; but I preferred getting out to
look round the little church. They were busy
with preparations for a funeral, and I inquired
the name of the deceased person for whom
these honours were intended. M. de Bussières replied, " It is one of my friends, Count
de Laferronnays; his sudden death is the
cause of the depression of spirits you may
have observed in me the last day or two."

I did not know M. de Laferronnays, I had
never even seen him; and so I felt nothing
more than that vague kind of sorrow which
one always feels at hearing of a sudden death.
M. de Bussières left me to make some arrangements about the tribune that was to
be set apart for the family of the deceased.
" I shall not tax your patience long," said
he; " I shall not be away more than a few
minutes."

The church of S. Andrea delle Fratte is
small, poor, and almost deserted; I think I
was almost the only person in it, and there
was no work of art to attract my attention.

I was looking round mechanically, without
any definite thought or purpose; I remember only a black dog, which bounded and
jumped before me as I moved about. . . .
Suddenly the dog disappeared, the whole
church disappeared; I saw nothing further, . . . or rather, O my God, I saw one
only object!

And how should I speak of it? Ah, no,
no words of man can even attempt to utter
the unutterable; all description, how sublime
soever, must of necessity be only a degradation of the ineffable reality.

I lay there, prostrate, bathed in tears, my
heart completely absorbed and lost, when
M. de Bussières recalled me to life. I could
not answer his eager hurried questions; but
at length I grasped the medal which I wore
in my bosom; I kissed with fervent emotion
the image of the Virgin, radiant with grace.
Oh, yes, it was indeed her very self!

I knew not where I was; I knew not
whether I was Alphonse Ratisbonne or not;
I was so entirely changed, that I did not know
myself. . . . I seemed to seek to identify myself, and to fail in the effort; . . . the most
glowing joy pervaded my heart; I could not
speak, I could reveal nothing; I felt within
me something so awful and so sacred, that I
asked for a priest. . . . I was taken to one, and
it was only at his positive command that I

spoke as well as I could, on my knees, and with a palpitating heart.

My first utterance was an expression of gratitude to M. de Laferronnays and to the Archconfraternity of Notre-Dame des Victoires. I knew intuitively that M. de Laferronnays had prayed for me.* I cannot tell how I knew it, any more than I can account for the truths of which I had suddenly gained both the knowledge and the belief. All I can say is, that the moment when the Blessed Virgin made a sign with her hand, the veil fell from my eyes; not one veil only, but all the veils which were wrapped around me disappeared, just as snow melts beneath the rays of the sun.

I came forth from a tomb, from an abyss of darkness; and I was living, perfectly, energetically living.... and yet I shed tears. I saw before me the fearful miseries from which I had been rescued by the mercy of God; I shuddered at the sight of my innumerable sins, and I was stupefied, melted, almost crushed by a sense of wonder and of gratitude.... I thought of my brother with a joy beyond words; but tears of compassion were

* M. de Laferronnays died suddenly on the evening of the 17th of January, 1842, after a life of edifying and consistent piety. The day before he had dined at Prince Borghese's, and M de Bussières had commended the young Jew, in whom he felt so much interested, to his prayers. M. de Laferronnays manifested a singular interest in this conversion.

mingled with my tears of love. Alas, that so
many should go quietly down into this yawn-
ing abyss with their eyes closed by pride or
by indifference ... should go down and be
swallowed up of this horrible darkness ... and
then, my family, my betrothed, my poor sisters! O torturing anxiety! My thoughts
were of you, O ye beloved ones,—my first
prayers were for you! ... And are you never
to raise your eyes towards the Saviour of the
world, whose blood hath blotted out original
sin? O, how foul is the blot of that stain!
how completely it obliterates every trace by
which we might recognise the creature that
was made in the image of God!

I am asked how I attained a knowledge of
these truths, since it is well known that I
never opened a religious book, had never read
a page of the Bible, and that the dogma of
original sin, which is either denied or utterly
forgotten by the modern Jews, had never for
a single moment occupied my thoughts,—
indeed, I doubt whether I had ever heard the
words which express it. How, then, did I
arrive at a knowledge of it? I know not. All
that I know is, that when I entered that
church I was profoundly ignorant of every
thing, and that when I came out I saw every
thing clearly and distinctly. The only explanation I can suggest is, that I was like a man
suddenly roused from slumber, or rather, like
a man born blind, whose eyes are suddenly

opened ;—he sees indeed, but he can give no
definition of that light which enlightens him,
and in which he beholds the objects of his
wondering gaze. And if we cannot explain
the light of nature, how should we be able to
explain that light which is in reality the very
truth itself? I think I state the precise truth
when I say that I knew not *the letter*, but that
I grasped fully the inner meaning and the
spirit of the Catholic dogmas. I rather *felt*
than *saw* them; and I felt them by the indescribable effects they produced within me.
The scene of these wonders was within, in my
soul; and their impressions, ten thousand
times more swift than thought, ten thousand
times deeper than reflection, had not only
shaken my soul to its foundation, but had, as
it were, turned it round, and given it another
direction, towards another end, and in the
power of a new life.

I know I am expressing my meaning very
badly : but can you expect, monsieur, that I
should be able to measure with narrow and
dry speech those emotions which my heart
itself could with difficulty contain?

But however inexact and imperfect these
my words may be, the simple fact of the case
is, that I found myself in some sort like a
bare and naked being; my soul was a *tabula
rasa.* .... The world had no longer any existence for me ; my prejudices against Christianity were no more; the instincts and pre-

possessions of my childhood were gone, and had left no trace; the love of my God had so entirely ejected and replaced every other love, that my betrothed herself appeared to me in quite another light: I loved her as one might love any object which God held within His outstretched hands, as a precious gift which yet more endears the giver.

I repeat that I implored my confessor, Father Villefort, and M. de Bussières to observe an inviolable secrecy in regard of what had happened to me. My earnest wish was to bury myself in a Trappist monastery, and occupy myself exclusively with the things of eternity; and, besides, I confess I thought that my family and my friends would deem me crazed—that they would turn me into ridicule; and that it was better for me in every way to escape entirely from the world —from its opinions and its judgments.

However, my ecclesiastical superiors showed me that this ridicule, reproach, and false judgments were but a part of that chalice which is put to the lips of every real Christian; they urged me not to decline this chalice, and told me how Jesus Christ had predicted to His disciples, sufferings, torments, and anguish. These solemn and pregnant word were, so far from discouraging me, that they increased my interior joy; I felt myself ready and prepared for every thing, and I eagerly craved baptism. They wished to

interpose some delay : " but," I exclaimed,
" those Jews who heard the preaching of the
Apostles were baptised immediately, and you
wish to put me off, after I have heard the
Queen of Apostles ! " My deep emotion, my
vehement desire, my repeated supplications
touched the hearts of these holy men ; and I
was consoled by the blessed promise of an
early baptism.

I could scarcely await the day fixed upon
for the fulfilment of this promise, so foul and
deformed I felt myself before God ; and yet,
what kindness, what love was lavished on me
during those days of my preparation ! I was
admitted into the house of the Jesuits, to
make a retreat under Father Villefort's direction ; and he fed and gladdened my soul with
the most delightful and soothing utterances
of the Divine Word. That man of God can
hardly be called a man ; he is rather all heart,
—a personification of heavenly charity. But
no sooner were my eyes opened, than I saw
around me many, many men of similar stamp,
of whose existence the world knows nothing.
What gentle kindness, what delicacy, what
gracefulness, have I found in my intercourse
with these Christians indeed ! During my retreat, the venerable superior of the Jesuits
visited me every evening, and poured the
fragrant balm of heaven into my soul. He
spoke to me but a few words ; but they were
words which expanded and grew as I listened

11

to them, and filled me with joy and light and life.

That priest, so humble, and yet so powerful, had no need to speak to me; it was enough to see him: the remembrance of his features is even now enough to place me in the presence of God, and to make my whole soul glow with living gratitude. I cannot find words to express all my gratitude; I should need a thousand tongues to tell the love I feel for these men of God,—for M. Theodore de Bussières, that minister and forerunner of Mary—for the family of the Laferronnays, whom I regard with a veneration and an affection above all words.

At length the 31st of January dawned upon me, and I found myself surrounded with an atmosphere of tenderness and sympathy. How gladly would I know each one of those pious souls, that I might express my fervent gratitude! May they all ever pray for me, even as I pray for them!

O Rome, what grace and blessing have I found in thy sacred bosom! The Mother of my Lord and Saviour had arranged all that concerned me; she had brought a French priest to address me in my mother-tongue at the solemn moment of my baptism,—I mean M. Dupanloup, whose memory is linked indissolubly to that of the most profound emotions of my life. Happy they whose privilege it was to listen to him; for the echoes of that

mighty address which the press has repeated
can give no idea of what it really was. I
felt that he too was inspired by her of whom
he was speaking.

I will not relate the circumstances of my
baptism, my confirmation, and my first communion,—suffice it to say, that I received all
these ineffable graces in that one day at the
hands of his Eminence Cardinal Patrizi vicar
of his Holiness.

I should weary you, were I to attempt to
tell you of all my impressions,—of all that I
have seen and heard and felt. . . . if I were
to make mention of the brotherly charity
which has been so profusely lavished on me.
I will mention only the very distinguished
Cardinal Mezzofanti ; . . . . the Lord has en-
dowed this illustrious person with the gift of
tongues, in reward of a heart which makes
itself every thing to every one.

One last great consolation was in reserve
for me. You remember how earnestly I
wished to see the Holy Father; indeed this
desire, or this curiosity, had kept me at
Rome longer than I intended. Little did I
imagine under what circumstances my wish
was to be gratified. It was as a new-born
child of the Church that I was presented to the
Father of all the faithful. From the moment
of my baptism I had felt for the Sovereign
Pontiff the reverent love of a son ; and I was
delighted when it was told me that I was to

be introduced into his presence by the reverend General of the Jesuits. Yet I trembled
at the anticipation, for I had never mingled
with great people; and the earth's greatest
men sunk into insignificance in presence of
this true greatness. I confess that all the
royalties of earth seemed to me concentrated
upon the head of him who wields on earth the
powers of the world to come; upon that
pontiff who succeeds in an unbroken line, to
the keys of St. Peter, and to the high-priest-
hood of Aaron,—that representative of Jesus
Christ himself, whose unshaken throne he fills.

Never shall I forget my awe and the beat-
ings of my heart as I entered the Vatican,
and passed through the vast courts, the imposing halls, which led to the sanctuary of
the Pontiff. But all my anxiety was dis-
pelled, to make room for surprise and wonder,
when I saw him himself, so simple, so humble,
so paternal. He was not a monarch, but a
father, whose extreme kindness treated me as
a beloved son.

My God! and will it be thus at that last
day, when I shall appear before Thee, to give
account of all the graces I have received?
We tremble at thought of the majesty of
God, and we fear His justice; but when His
mercy shall be made known, our hopes and
trust will revive, and with them a love and a
gratitude without bounds.

Gratitude? yes, gratitude is henceforward

my law and my life. Never can I adequately express it in words; but I will endeavour to condense and suggest it by my actions.

The letters I have received from my family set me free from every engagement; and I offer my liberty to God, for all my life, to be employed in the service of the Church and of my brethren, under the protection of Mary. . . .

11*

THE LATTER YEARS

OF

M. LE COMTE DE LAFERRONNAYS.

WE feel it a duty to append to the narrative of this wonderful conversion two letters written to the *Union Catholique*, containing a brief account of the latter years of the Count de Laferronnays, whose name is so closely connected with that of M. Ratisbonne.

Rome, 19th January, 1842.

As you go along the Via Sacra, amongst the monuments which surround the ancient Forum with their picturesque ruins, you will notice that the temple of the twin-founders of Rome has suffered less than the rest from the ravages of time, and of the barbarian invaders of Rome. Christianity consecrated it, and so preserved its ruins. It was restored by a Pope in the sixth century; and became a church under the invocation of St. Cosmas and St. Damian—two brothers also, two Christian brothers, united during life by their mutual love, in death by martyrdom, in eternity by a common glory.

I love this church, as a monument of the earlier triumphs of the faith over paganism. Yesterday the Blessed Sacrament was exposed in it, and I went to visit it. My mind was full of the memory of M. de Laferronnays; and I was thinking that, but a year ago, he was kneeling near me in that church, praying at the tomb of the two martyrs, in presence of the Blessed Sacrament. I pictured him to myself as I had seen him, kneeling at the balustrade of the sanctuary, in an attitude of deep recollection, with his hands clasped, and his features composed into an angelic fervour. I read over again, with deep feeling, a prayer of reparation composed by him and written with his own hand, which he had let fall from his book as he was going away...... His death allows me to publish this touching prayer; and I think you will be glad to see some extracts from it. Surely it is for the glory of God; and it reveals to us the grandeur of his own soul and the fervour of his true repentance:

"O mysterious provision of a love surpassing knowledge, it is to Thee I owe my rescue from despair; Thou alone couldst, and Thou didst raise my soul out of the deadly despondency into which it was cast by the appalling and ever-present memory of my numberless and heinous sins...... I may show myself to the world as a living proof of Thine inexhaustible and most tender pity. I confess

that, during the frightful madness to which 1
willingly abandoned myself for so many years.
I have exceeded the extremest limits of ingra-
titude. From my childhood Thou hadst made
me feel Thy protection, in placing me under
the shield and direction of the tenderest and
most pious of mothers, until the age when I
was first called and admitted to Thy holy table. And still later, when my passions began
to lay on me their degrading yoke, Thou, O
my God, didst not cease to call me to Thyself.
Often, amidst my wanderings. Thy voice
reached my heart's depth in spite of all my
resistance, and there uttered its severe counsels, its salutary threatenings; but, alas, Thy
paternal admonitions did not lead me to repentance; they occasioned only transitory
uneasiness, which I shook off by plunging yet
deeper into sin. Later still, when Thou didst
allow my lot to be united to that of the most
excellent of women, Thou didst surround me
with patterns and guides, who all pointed out
to me the way of return unto Thee by walking
in it themselves so faithfully. It is Thou, O
God of goodness, who hast constantly and
strangely preserved me during all the vicissi-
tudes of my public life! In those days of revolution and wild folly, my sullied soul could
have appeared before the tribunal of Thy justice only to hear the sentence of its everlasting condemnation. Thou didst allow death
to threaten, but not to strike, my guilty head;

Thou didst wait still for my love! And these
are but the least of the graces Thou hast bestowed on me; and how have I recompensed
them!..... For more than half a century I
have wilfully closed my eyes, that I might
not see, and stopped my ears, that I might
not hear. I sacrificed to the devil my rest, my
life, my conscience, my soul, my salvation.
Regardless of thy goodness, O my God, and
putting away the Hand that was stretched
out to save me, I took pleasure in accumulat-
ing sin upon sin, outrage upon outrage, as
though I were eagerly bent on my own de-
struction. My iniquities towered like a great
mountain up to the throne of Thy justice, and
braved and provoked Thy vengeance......
O my God, never, never was any child of
Thine so ungrateful, so guilty as I then was
in Thy sight. And when at length, sated and
palled with the poisoned pleasures of the
world, exhausted by weariness and disgust, tho
snows of old age brought their warnings of
death,—when serious thoughts and an awak-
ening sorrow shook my soul,—then, horrified
at myself, I thought my hour of forgiveness
was past, that my tardy and insufficient remorse could no more disarm Thine anger:
and I added to all my other sins this greatest
sin—I doubted Thy mercy. But Thou didst
send to my aid a guide, a comforter, who sus-
tained my courage, and led me to Thy feet,

and taught me to know Thee better, to im-
plore Thy forgiveness and to hope."

Do not these pages, marked as they are
by the tears of M. de Laferronnays, seem
as though they were taken from that book
in which St. Augustine, touched by God's
grace, has treasured up the confession of
his long wanderings, and the bitter expression of his regrets?

In one of his letters he gives an account
of his conversion. We give it in his own
words; for who would presume to substi-
tute a narrative for these touching effusions
of a penitent soul at the foot of the cross?

"The reflections I have had time enough
to make during my long and lonely journey,
have at length borne some fruit. When I
reached Paris, I was convinced, and my
mind was made up; my decision and my
conviction are not the result of enthusiasm
or of precipitation. Nor is it the brilliance of
any light that might dazzle me that has
opened my eyes : my soul has not been compelled to put itself on the defensive against
the charm of a persuasive eloquence; whatever living convictions I have ever had
spring from within me. I have yielded only
after long and earnest resistance; the old
man has struggled vigorously—the conflict
has been long and desperate. But as I re-
traced my eight-and-fifty years, and exam-
ined calmly the long succession of days

which were employed in sin ; as I thought of
the evil example I had given to others, and the
scandal of which I have so often been the occasion ; as I reflected that amongst this countless
multitude of actions there was not one that
was good,—I was horrified at myself, and conceived such a detestation of myself, that
despair had well-nigh seized my heart, to
the exclusion of true repentance. I passed
several days of my journey in a state of
violent and painful emotion. Then, all on
a sudden, I know not how or why, I felt
myself calm and almost happy, as though
some gentle and soothing influence had sunk
down into my soul. It was hope. I remem-
bered that hope was not only permitted, but
commanded as a duty, and that forgiveness
was promised to the penitent sinner. I
blessed and praised God for having awakened my conscience, and for soothing my
remorse by hope and faith. And in this
state of mind I reached Paris. I felt now
that I have no more to dread human respect, no more false shame to overcome.
One of my first visits was paid to your
friend in the Rue de Grenelle, to whom I
gave your letter. I had a long interview
with him. I was anxious that *the man*
should know *the man* before *the judge* heard
the tale of *the culprit*. I told him all the
story of my sinful life; and I assure you I
did it sincerely, and without any conscious

desire to exculpate myself. I felt a kind of
comfort and of ease in thus giving him my
confidence, even without imposing on him
any obligation of secrecy; it seemed to me
a fitting and useful penance. After these con-
fessions made to the man, it was neither painful nor difficult to me to repeat them at the
feet of the judge who has received the noble
mission, the consoling power, to pardon and
to absolve. My habitual vanity made a faint
resistance, but a better feeling vanquished it;
and I have a good hope that God, who reads
all hearts, saw my sincere repentance, and
that His infinite mercy has ratified the sentence of His minister. And now ten days
have passed. I feel with delight and with
gratitude that my resolutions are stronger day
by day. My reason, subjugated by grace,
humbly accepts the teaching of faith; my understanding no longer loses itself in vain and
fruitless analyses of mysteries beyond its
range; I believe in all simplicity, and I find
it a blessing and a boon to be able to believe
that which commands nothing but what is
good, and promises nothing but happiness."

This was a great and solemn crisis in the
life of Count de Laferronnays. Having once
resolved, he never wavered, but steadily per-
severed. Nothing could throw him back, or
quell his courage. He *believed*, and from
that moment his whole life was raised up to
the high level of his faith. The terrors of

human respect, which are generally so mighty in public men, never shook his noble heart. It was so high a blessedness, so great an honour, as he said, to possess the Catholic faith, that he could not but walk manfully erect in its divine light. While he was as humble and simple as a child in all his prac-tices of devotion, his soul grasped and held with a generous fervour the loftiest inspira-tions of Christianity. He felt and realised all its strong resolves, all its tender yet energetic emotions, its meek compassion, its sublime self-devotedness, its high thoughts, its far-reaching views, its rarest and choicest sug-gestions. Certainly his was a grand and a noble soul; and religion, in pervading him with its mighty life, had still further raised and ennobled him.

. I do not affect, however, to pronounce his eulogy; I wish you simply to see him as he really was. Here is an extract from a letter written in reference to a friend who had lost his only child, a tenderly-beloved daughter: "What a wretched return home! What a moment was their arrival at L——*without her!* What a void around them, within them; and what a despoiled and desolate life is theirs! All these thoughts oppress the heart and weary the mind, and lay him who has the blessedness of believing prostrate at the foot of the cross. What can we ask or expect of man in these great crises of the soul!

12

How can the most quick and tender sympathy reach a grief so poignant? No, my
dear friend, the deepest affection is powerless
here; it can find no words to heal a wound
like this. Religion alone, and unfailingly,
suggests the words which the smitten heart
craves to hear; it alone has the right and the
power to take from our tears their excess of
bitterness; it alone dares speak of hope in
presence of despair; it alone can tell of a
compensating future to those who have no
longer either past or present. Religion alone
has the sublime power to raise from the dust
the stricken soul, by speaking of the certainty
of the eternal reunion of those whom death's
fell stroke has for awhile sundered. O, how
I pity those who suffer, and yet are so miserable as to feel any doubt on these grand and
comforting truths! Whenever a fresh grief
assails the heart, how sad not to know where
to look for succour; to be obliged to wrestle
with anguish and with despair *alone*. The
soul of the Christian, on the contrary, fix is
ever a sure refuge at the foot of the cross;
there it pours forth its tears, and the wail of its
grief: thence it draws the strength and the courage of resignation, which is simply impossible without the faith which gives hope...."

The same grace which had led him to the
true source of consolation, revealed to him
also the value and worth in the eyes of God
of those souls which sin has degraded, and

which the Christian faith can restore, while
the world crushes them with its scorn. What
striking words are these, in reference to a
distinguished person, who was drawing near
to the close of a life of most shameful disorder:
"That head once so high, so insolent,—
now bowed down to the grave; that countenance, so witty, so merry, so boldly bad in
its expression,—now so gloomy, so besotted,
and all its fire extinguished! All this slow
and humiliating decomposition of a form and
a constitution which was the matter of so
much pride, the instrument and incentive of
such daring abuses! What lessons are these!
Well, my friend, this decrepitude, this moral
death, this loathsome close of a scandalous
life disgusts the world; it flees in horror, or
contempt, or pity. But God is there still.
He judges not as men judge; with one word,
with one look, He can raise again that degraded soul, and renew and sanctify it. And
he, whom we look upon with so much disdain, with a pity so insulting—could he but
once raise his heart and his eyes to heaven—
this man, so worn out by sin, has perhaps his
prepared place on high! Yet a few days of
suffering and of humiliation, and it may be
he will look down on us with pity and compassion! Our sublime religion teaches us
thus much; and these people, forsooth, tell
you that it is mere foolery! They kill you,
they wither and waste you, and then give

you up to annihilation; and they call this
philosophy, the love of wisdom ! "

The ambition of M. de Laferronnays had
never been tempted by the glitter of greatness, nor by the desire of playing an important part in those councils on which hung
suspended the destiny of France and of all
Europe. He wrote thus, on the very day of
his nomination to the Ministry of Foreign
Affairs :

"My friend, I am very wretched and
very unfortunate. In spite of all my resolutions, I have accepted this dreaded office.
I might, perhaps, have resisted the wishes of
the king ; but I have yielded to his sadness,
to his goodness ; and here I am, chained to
the oar. You will read my sentence this
morning in the *Moniteur ;* and you will be
able to say to yourself that, even in my new
position, coveted as it is by so many, France
does not contain a more pitiable and unfortunate creature than I am. It is a singular
thing, this destiny,—and I can make nothing
of mine ; for it drives me always in the direc
tion I am anxious to avoid. But it has never
behaved so badly, never played me such a
trick as this. If ever you happen to hear
that I am ambitious, that I love what men
call honours, and the whirl and bustle of business, and the importance of a great place, or
any of those great human absurdities in virtue
of which men worry one another, and over-

turn empires, pray make haste and tell them it is all false."

But it was from a graver and loftier point of view that he looked down upon these *human absurdities* after his conversion. He was raised above them by all the height of that eternity which was his habitual thought.

" When it is at the close of fifty years of life that these grand thoughts of death and its results lay hold on one, do you think it well to try to distract one's mind, and that one is wrong in not feeling disposed to make the attempt? Will you deem me very absurd in desiring that nothing may ever lessen the influence of these thoughts upon me,— thoughts which are most mighty and influential in silence and in solitude? No, my friend, I am very sure that you understand me ; and that if any imperious duty compelled me to give it my feeble remnant of strength, you would be able to pity me, and to appreciate the immense sacrifice which it would be to me at my age, and with such a terrible past. Every moment is of infinite value ; one fears every thing that might divert or alter the employment of these precious moments. I have lost so much time, that every thing which stops me on my way, or throws me back, may expose me to the risk of being surprised before I reach my goal. Perhaps I am too singular in all this; the politicians of your *salons*, and your editors

12*

of journals, don't think of these things; and in urging me as they do, they care very little where I should fall at the last. But it is of great importance to me. And so they may rest assured that, unless I feel convinced that it is the will of God concerning me, no considerations will induce me to yield."

Most of the admirable letters were written from Rome. It was at Rome, that pure source of the faith, that this noble soul had drunk in the copious dews of heaven, and struck its roots so deep in so short a time; it was in the genial warmth of that Catholic atmosphere that it had opened its loveliest flowers, and diffused its most fragrant perfumes. And it was on that hallowed soil, which he had found so propitious to him, that the venerable tree fell, almost pressed to earth by the weight of its fruit,—its tender charity, its sincere and unaffected piety, its lowly repentance, and all the other graces of which his vigorous old age, renewed by faith, had been so fruitful. And the sweet odour of his sanctity abides in the Church of Rome, as an added glory and adornment; in the memory of all his friends, as a powerful charm which binds them or draws them to Christianity; and in the very hearts he has bruised so sore, as a balm of heaven to their wounds, as a manifest pledge of eternal life.

Rome, 29th January, 1842.

I had gathered the details enclosed herewith a few days after the death of M. de Laferronnays. By some unhappy inadvertence, the letter, which I thought was on its way to you, was left in my desk. I still forward it, notwithstanding the delay which I deplore; the memory of M. de Laferronnays cannot be so soon effaced in France, even in these lively times when an event can scarcely preserve a past of twenty-four hours. . . . .

Alas, alas, another grievous loss, a loss quite unexpected too! The day before yesterday, at this very hour, my old and dear friend, Count de Laferronnays, was with me to introduce a young painter whose genius and piety had inspired him with a lively interest. When I reproached him for being late, he said: "I could not come sooner; I had an important letter to write, and it was indispensable that it should go off to-day. . . . " He little thought, nor did I, how indispensable it was that he should avail himself of that courier. I left him to pay some visits, without bidding him adieu even; and I was never to see him again alive. . . . . He accompanied my children, who were going out with his daughter, and his son-in law, the Count de Meun; they went together to St. John

Lateran, where he prayed for a considerable
time before the Blessed Sacrament, as was
his wont. He complained a little of a pain in
the chest, which came on at intervals, and was
so sharp and sudden that it prevented his
walking; but in all other respects he was as
cheerful and lively as usual. My children
met him again at Benediction, in the chapel
at the Perpetual Adoration, on the Quirinal.

There was on that evening a brilliant *fête*
at the Austrian Embassy. Madame de Laferronnays was to take her daughters there;
and while they were dressing, M. de Laferronnays amused himself by playing with his
grandchild. It was between half-past eight
and nine; he complained still of his pain; but
as it was habitual, they were sorry for it, but
felt no serious anxiety. They attributed it to
the effect of a *brasero* they had put into the
room to warm it, and the excessive heat of
which had drawn the blood to his chest. But,
however that may have been, they sent for
the physician. Madame de Laferronnays
wrote a few words to the Abbé Gerbet; but
his state occasioned so little alarm, that M. de
Menn expressed to his sister-in-law his regret
at Madame de Laferronnays' tendency to
exaggerate her husband's ailments. The letter
to the Abbé Gerbet was not sent immediately.
When the physician arrived, he advised bleeding, and a surgeon was sent for. But the pain
became easier; they thought the crisis past,

and stopped the bleeding. However, the return of the pain made them send again for the surgeon, who made two fruitless attempts to bleed him again. He now suffered most acutely, and cries of anguish escaped him in spite of his self-control. During this time, his wife —his angelic wife—was in a state of keen distress; going and coming, trying to avoid hearing his moans; when a few words disclosed to her the imminence of the danger. She sat down by the bed on which he had just been laid, took his hand in hers, and did not leave him again. She sat in perfect calmness, full of gentleness and resignation. Meanwhile the Abbé Gerbet arrived, approached the bed, and gave him his blessing; and then, at some questions addressed to him, the beloved patient replied with a surprising burst of fervour: " Yes, yes; oh, yes, I do repent of all my sins. Oh, yes, I do love God with all my soul!" And taking the crucifix, he pressed it eagerly to his lips, and repeated several times this simple invocation: " My God, have mercy on me! Holy Virgin, pray for me; come to my aid!" He had enjoyed the privilege of communicating the day before. In this extreme danger his confessor gave him absolution; he received it with profound repentance, and his eyes were blinded with tears of sorrow and of gratitude. Then his face regained its usual serenity, and betokened the calmness, the divine peace, the heavenly joy of his soul.

" How happy I feel now!" said he, with fail-
ing voice, but with a smile of absolute confidence and hope; "how happy I feel now!"
But soon his breathing became more difficult:
"Adieu," said he to his beloved wife, taking
her hand in his, "adieu, my dear children!"...
and in a few moments his soul, so pure, so
noble, so truly Christian, appeared before
God; while his young daughters were kneeling beside his bed in their gay festival dresses.

It was a heart-rending scene. It was now
only half-past ten o'clock. What an unexpected bereavement! what a thunder-stroke!
But this sudden death, which snapped in two
hours bonds so strong and so sweet, came not
unlooked-for by him whom it smote. For many
years he had been awaiting his summons, and
prepared himself every day for death, as
though each day were certainly his last. On
that very day he had said to his wife, on his
return home : " I have been to Sta. Maria Maggiore. I knelt down, and implored the Ma-
donna; and I said to God : Behold me, O
Lord, I am ready : take me if Thou willest to
have me; but if Thou permittest me to remain
yet longer on earth, my life shall be consecrated to thy glory alone! " The thought of
death had become habitual to him, yet it did
not ruffle the deep calmness of his heart, or
affect the simple gentle gaiety of his conversation; a profound distaste for pleasures and
honours had detached him from those illusions

of which he had felt all the nothingness, and
the energy of his faith disclosed to him,
beyond the grave, the only hopes which could
fill and content his magnificent soul. Rome,
with the solemn associations of its ruins, deepened the tone of those grave and holy
thoughts which were most congenial to him.
I have before me a letter which he wrote
nearly a year ago; a few extracts from it will
reveal to you his habitual state of mind :
"I leave Rome with regret; and but for
the important matters which summon me to
France, I should certainly have prolonged my
stay. I suppose it is because I see it now
with other eyes, and feel more deeply all its
significance. For him who is blessed with
faith, for him who has ever held lonely con-
verse with himself in that city of silence and
of faith, Rome is the city to live and to die
in. I admire as much as any one these co-
lossal ruins, which give one so grand an idea
of what ancient Rome must have been, and of
the wonderful people who raised them. I can
well understand why the imagination should
be at once enthralled and excited amidst these
stately relics; yet it is not the ruins which
fascinate me, nor the recollections of olden
time which make me sorry to leave it. It is
the soil of those theatres moistened with the
blood of thousands of martyrs, the precious
remains of those heroes of the faith, which are

here preserved and venerated on the very
spot of their glorious agony; it is the sacred
dust of the catacombs, that hallowed ground
which has witnessed the sufferings and the
triumphs of the Church, its tribulations
and its glories; it is that unshaken rock,
against which the impotent efforts of impiety,
heresy, and philosophism, have been broken
and thrown back, age after age,—this throne
of the poor fisherman, set up on the ruins of
the throne of the Cæsars, the rulers of the
world! And all that is here, all around me
as I walk. O my friend, how can one see all
this, and not believe? how can one help feeling at Rome some presentiment of our eternal
destiny? how can we miss seeing whence our
souls came, and whither they are going?
How can people come to Rome only to see
lifeless stones? Above all, how can they have
the heart, when surrounded by so many witnesses of God and of His power, of the Catholic religion and its truth,—how can they
stoop to petty criticisms of incidental abuses,
of the political state of the country, or of the
peculiarity of certain religious usages and ceremonies—ceremonies and usages of which
our little minds know neither the meaning
nor the necessity? To a Catholic soul Rome
is simply Catholic Rome; it is the land of
Catholic memorials, of Catholic miracles, of
Catholic hopes. Here one's faith grows

stronger ; here the Catholic raises a corner of
that veil which shrouds the sublime mysteries
of our religion ; here the heart of the Catholic
sees with a clear and distinct intuition the
vanity and nothingness of the pomps and
glories of this world, and already breathes the
calm and genial atmosphere of the unvarying
eternity. I saw Rome three times while my
heart was yet frozen in religious indifference ;
and being neither an artist nor a poet, I was
terribly tired,—just as one grows tired of a
long harangue in an unknown tongue. But
now I have the faculty which enables me to
see, to hear, to understand, to feel. My days
are all too short, I am so eager to see and to
know every thing. My soul is filled with
most delightful emotions—emotions which are
the more living and exquisite that they are so
new and fresh to me. May God grant that I
may once again see Rome.... Yes, it is at
Rome I would fain live and die...."
    And God heard his prayer. The Count
de Laferronnays did return to Rome ; he lived
there amid all the aids and consolations of
the faith, and he died amidst all its graces
and benedictions.
    His death occasioned many sorrows and
many tears. He was so affectionate and so
gentle, that he was loved by every one.
Cunctorum amans, cunctis amabilissimus.
His body was embalmed, and lay in state
13

three days in the Palazzo Spina. Many pre-
lates and priests of France made it a point to
say Mass in that quiet chapel. The venerable
Father de Geramb passed a whole night in
prayer beside his bier—last and deepest expression of a friendship begun in youthful
dissipation, sanctified afterwards by that religion which had made the one a pattern of
true piety in the world, and the other a
model of austerities and of penitence in a
cloister of La Trappe. Every homage that
could honor his memory and comfort his
bereaved family was paid to his remains.
His own numerous friends, many illustrious for-
eigners, the ambassadors of France, Austria,
and Naples, and crowds of noble women, who
prayed and mourned apart, formed the glorious procession of his funeral. The sorrow
of all these sympathising souls was soothed
by an extraordinary event connected with
this sudden death. The day after, in that
very church, and a few steps only from the
bier prepared for his funeral, M. Alphonse
Ratisbonne, for whose conversion he had
breathed his latest prayers, was smitten down
like St. Paul by a supernatural vision, and
arose imploring holy baptism, and blessing the
memory of the illustrious deceased, who had
prayed for him without knowing him. Thus
God Himself seemed to authorise us to believe
the everlasting blessedness of the soul of our

beloved friend ; for while we were here on
earth offering our tears, our prayers, and the
precious blood of Jesus Christ for his repose,
the power of his intercession in heaven was
attested in our midst by a miracle !

THE END.

PUBLICATIONS OF P. J. KENEDY,

EXCELSIOR

Catholic Publishing House,

5 BARCLAY ST., Near Broadway,

Opposite the Astor House,   NEW YORK.

All for the Sacred Heart of Jesus. Dedicated to asso-
    ciates of Leag . of Sacred Heart. Net............   50
Adelmar the Tem . r, a Tale of the Crusades.........   .40
Adventures and D ring Deeds of Michael Dwyer......   1.00
All about Knock. Complete account of Cures, etc.....   1.00
Apparitions and Miracles at Knock, paper cover.......   .25
Atala. By Chateaubriand. Doré's Illustrations, 4to gilt   3.00
Battle of Ventry Harbor, paper cover..................   .20
Bible, Douay. Octavo, large print. Vellum cloth....   2.50
    The same, American Morocco, gilt edges.,.........   5.00
    The same, Turkey Morocco, antique, gilt edges....   10.00
Bible, Haydock's, Style G.Fr. Morocco paneled, 2 clasps. 18.00
    The same, Style H., Turkey Morocco beveled.....   25.00
Bianche, or the great evils of Pride. 40
Blind Agnese, Little Spouse of the Blessed Sacramen .   .50
British Catholic Poets, red line, gilt edges 25
Brooks (Senator) and Hughes (Archbishop) Controversy.   .75
Burke's Lectures and Sermons 1st series, cloth........   2.00
    The same, full gilt side and edges,...............   3.00
Burke's Lectures and Sermons, 2d series cloth.......   2.00
    The same, full gilt side and edges................   3.00
Burke's Lectures and Sermons in Ireland, cloth.......   2.50
    The same, full gilt side and edges. 3.00
Burke's Lectures—The set complete, 3 vols, plain......   6.00
    The same gilt...................................   9.00
Burke's Reply to Froude, Ireland's case stated........   1.00
Cannon's Poems and Dramas. Red line, gilt edges...   1.25

Catholic Prayer-Books, 25c., 50c., up to 12 00
    Any of above books sent free by mail on receipt of
price. Agents wanted everywhere to sell above books, to
whom liberal terms will be given. Address
P. J. KENEDY, Excelsior Catholic Publishing
    House, 5 Barclay Street, New York.

Publications of P. J. Kenedy, 5 Barclay St. N. Y.

Canon Schmid's Exquisite Tales, 6 vols, Illustrated... 3.00
Cannon's Practical Spelling Book .... .25
Captain of the Club, a Story for Boys................... .75
Carroll O'Donoghue. By Christine Faber............... 1.25
Carpenter's Speller and Definer...................... .25
Catechism Third Plenary Council, large, No. 2, paper..
   per 100 net ... ...,.... .... 4.50
   The same, abridged No. 1, paper per 100 net... 1.50
   The same, No. 2, cloth flexible, per 100 net.... 6.00
   The same, No 1,   "   "   "   "   "....... 8.50
Catechism, General, National Council, paper per 100 net. 2.00
   The same, abridged paper cover, per 100 net........ 1.50
Catechism, Butler's large, paper per 100 net..... ...... 2.50
   The same, abridged, paper per 100 net...... .... 1.50
   The same, cloth, Illustrated Mass Prayers......... .30
Catechism, The, or Short abridgment, New York, per
   100 net...................................... 2.00
Catechism, Boston. Prayers at Mass, etc., paper per
   100 net.. 2.00
Catechism, Keenan's Doctrinal, cloth............... :.... .50
Catechism, Poor Man's, large and thick. .... .40
Catechism, Spanish, Ripalda, paper cover............. 12
Catechism, Spanish, Astete, paper cover.. .... .15
Catechism, Spanish, Nuevo Caton, paper cover........ .15
Catholic Christian Instructed, paper .20, cloth........... .30
Catholic Excelsior Library, 6 vols, per set............. 4.50
Catholic Faith and Morals, By L'Homond............. 1.00
Catholic Fireside Library, 10 vols, per set.. .... 7.50
Catholic Flowers from Protestant Gardens, gilt.. ..... 1.25
Catholic Home Library, 8 vols, per set..... .... 4.00
Catholic Juvenile Library, 6 vols, per set...... ,.... 2.40
Catholic Keepsake Library, 6 vols, per set.......... 4.50
Catholic Missions and Missionaries. By Shea... ...... 2.50
Catholic Offering or Gift Book. By Abp. Walsh ..... *.00
Catholic Piety, (Prayer Book). Prices range upwards
   from.. ..... ,.... .... .60
Catholic School Book..... .... .25
Chambers' English Literature, 2 vols, Octavo.......... 5.00

Catholic Prayer-Books, 25c., 50c., up to 12 00
☞ Any of above books sent free by mail on receipt of
price. Agents wanted everywhere to sell above books, to
whom liberal terms will be given. Address
P. J. KENEDY, Excelsior Catholic Publishing
House, 5 Barclay Street, New York.

Publications of P. J. Kenedy, 5 Barclay St. N. Y.

Chancellor and his Daughter. Sir Thos. More....... 1.25
Christian Etiquette. For Ladies and Gentlemen....... 1.25
Christian Maiden's Love. By Louis Veuillot. .... .75
Christian's Rule of Life. By St. Liguori............. .50
Christian Virtues. By St. Liguori 1.00
Christopher Columbus. Illustrated, 4to gilt........... 3.00
Chivalrous Deed. By Christine Faber....... ...... 1.25
Clifton Tracts Library of Controversy, 4 vols... .... 3.00
Collins' Poem Red line, gilt edge................... 1.25
Converted Jew. M. A. Ratisbonne... 50
Countess of Glosswood.... .... .75
Crown of Jesus (Prayer Book). Prices range upwards
  from... ... ... 1.00
Easy Companion (Prayer Book). Prices upwards from .25
Daily Piety, (Prayer Book). Prices upwards from.... .30
Dalaradia. By William Collins....... .... .75
Davis' Poems and Essays, complete 1.50
Devout Manual, 18mo, (Prayer Book). Prices upwards
  from.. 75
Devout Manual, 32mo, (Prayer Book). Prices upwards
  from.. . ... .35
Dick Massey, a Story of Irish Evictions........ .... 1.00
Diploma of Children of Mary Society, per 100 net..... 3.00
Doctrinal Catechism. By Rev. Stephen Keenan...... .50
Dove of the Tabernacle. By Rev. T. H. Kinane...... .75
Drops of Honey. By Father Zelus Animarum........ .75
Drops of Honey Library—9 volumes, per set.......... 6.75
Elevation of the soul to God............ .... .75
Empire and Papacy. The Money God 1.25
Epistles and Gospels, 24mo. Good Type............. .20
Erin go Bragh, Songster. Paper cover............... .25
Evenings at School. New edition Net... .... 1.00
Exercises of the Way of the Cross, paper cover ... ... .05
Faber's (Christine) Works, 4 vols, large, 12mo. per set. 5.00
Fair France during the Second Empire...... .... 1.00
Fair Maid of Connaught. By Mrs. Hughes..........' .75
Faugh a Ballagh Songster. Paper cover.............. .25
Feasts and Fasts. By Rev. Alban Butler. 1.25

Catholic Prayer-Books, 25c., 50c., up to 12 00
☞ Any of above books sent free by mail on receipt of
price. Agents wanted everywhere to sell above books, to
whom liberal terms will be given. Address
P J. KENEDY, Excelsior Catholic Publishing
  House, *5 Barclay Street, New York.*

Publications of P. J. Kenedy, 5 Barclay St. N. Y.

Catholic Prayer-Books, 25c., 50c., up to 12 00

☞ Any of above books sent free by mail on receipt of price. Agents wanted everywhere to sell above books, to whom liberal terms will be given. Address

P. J. KENEDY, Excelsior Catholic Publishing House, 5 Barclay Street, New York.

www.ingramcontent.com/pod-product-compliance
Lightning Source LLC
Chambersburg PA
CBHW020234030726
47497CB00009B/3093